WE
ARE
WOLVES

An anthology

Compiled by Gemma Amor, Laurel Hightower, and Cynthia Pelayo

Copyright

A Marriage of Dust and Blood by Michelle Garzon and Melissa Lason
Welcome Home by Jessica Guess
The Body You Loved by Gemma Amor

Presented by Burial Day Books

Cover art by Gemma Amor
Copy editing by Karmen Wells: www.shelfmadecreative.com
Cover formatting by: www.elderlemondesign.net
Editors: Gemma Amor, Laurel Hightower and Cynthia Pelayo

Print ISBN: 978-1-7356936-4-4
ebook ISBN: 978-1-7356936-5-1

TABLE OF CONTENTS

Praise for We Are Wolves

"The bravest book you'll read all year. Harrowing, yes, but necessarily so. As empowering as it is powerful. Not only does the book benefit a crucial cause, the stories are extraordinary, written by more than a dozen paramount voices in horror. Sometimes a book illuminates as it entertains; WE ARE WOLVES is that rare find."

Josh Malerman New York Times best-selling author of BIRD BOX and MALORIE

"Disturbing, evocative, and profoundly haunting, WE ARE WOLVES is a high-def snapshot of the future of the horror genre. It pulls no punches, asks for no quarter, and will leave you breathless.

I loved it."

Bestselling author and World Horror Grandmaster Award winner Brian Keene

"It takes a wolf to sing for wolves, and these stories sing in the dark. Gemma Amor, Laurel Hightower and Cina Pelayo invite readers to listen as varied writers' voices howl a shared, ferocious song."

Kathe Koja, Bram Stoker and Locus Award winning author of The Cipher and Velocities

"WE ARE WOLVES is a who's who of contemporary horror writers. This isn't an anthology about abuse; it's a collection of stories about survival, violence, vengeance, blood, and how women relentlessly push forward in a world that tries to maul them while asking them to smile. These women will tear you apart and hold you in their hands after because they are savage wolves, but also goddesses who understand pain, love, justice, and the importance of persistence."

Gabino Iglesias, author of Coyote Songs

"WE ARE WOLVES is a horror anthology with a viciously feminist bite. A startlingly horrific take on all that plagues the modern female; from sexism and assault, to the fraught and complicated role that is motherhood.

Compelling whilst challenging genre tropes along the way, this book will move you to stand up in solidarity with the women within its pages. Fast paced, twisted, and unapologetically female, WE ARE WOLVES is horror that simply can't be missed."

Meg Hafdahl, co-host of the Horror Rewind podcast and author of Twisted Reveries: Thirteen Tales of the Macabre, The Darkest Hunger, Daughters of Darkness, and Her Dark Inheritance, and co-author of The Science of Monsters, The Science of Women in Horror, and The Science of Stephen King

"The best nightmares are the ones that happen for the right reasons and this is one of the best reasons, and best collections of nightmares there is. Cina, Gemma and Laurel have assembled a flotilla of stories designed to terrify even as they assist, to entertain even as they carve their name onto every mirror. Help a good cause, run with the wolves. Howl with them."

Alasdair Stuart, professional enthusiast, pop culture analyst, writer behind the award-nominated weekly newsletter The Full Lid, Hugo finalist, and co-owner of the Escape Artists Podcast Network.

Foreword

I remember my assault.

I don't think about it on a day-to-day basis, and as life events go it doesn't consume my every waking thought, nor does it keep me up at night, not anymore. It certainly wasn't the worst thing that has ever happened to me, not by a long shot.

Which I suppose, now that I see that written down, is saying something isn't it?

But it was what I might call a Bad Thing, and the more distance I put between myself and the Bad Thing as the years roll by, the more I realise that it was, in fact, a Very Bad Thing. Our capacity to minimise the severity of Bad Things is limitless, it seems. I wonder where that comes from, that instinctive need to gloss over the terror or the hurt, to pull the smile-curtains tight across our faces and upon questioning, lie, endlessly lie: 'I'm fine!' We say, over and over, but many of us aren't. The lie pervades, the curtain hangs taut.

I certainly wasn't fine, but it took another woman to sit me down and tell me this, a day after the attack happened.

I had been out for the night with friends. I was walking home, full of booze and fondness for my nearest and dearest. I had jammed my headphones tight into my ears, because it was cold, and after midnight, and I wanted to get to my house as quickly as possible, and, just like it had done a hundred times before, I knew that music would get me there faster. I didn't cycle because my city is made of steep hills, and I didn't taxi because I believed it was a waste of money when my legs were perfectly good enough to get me where I needed to go.

I just walked, marching up a steep road called Nine Tree Hill, leaning into the gradient without a thought for my own safety or whereabouts, and then...the Bad Thing happened.

A split-second impression of something not quite right; of movement near me.

A sensation of speed, and closeness, and a gloved hand over my eyes, another over my mouth, arms encircling me from behind. Then, I was on the floor, and my bag was being ripped from my shoulder, and I tried to call out, receiving three sharp punches to my face and nose as reward, which rather effectively shut me up, silenced me. I've had a thing about silence, ever since. I resent it. Silence is control, silence is the transference of power from one individual to another, and I reject it wholeheartedly.

Fuck silence.

When I felt feet kicking at my ribs, I realised with horror that there were two assailants, not one, and that realisation made me afraid. Before, there hadn't been room for fear, only bewilderment. Now there was a sudden understanding that my entire body was at risk, and that fear was the most profound I had ever felt, and that would remain the case until I gave birth to my son.

But, that's enough about that.

Because what stayed with me longer than the balaclava-toting bogeymen who left ring prints on the side of my nose and bruises on my ribcage were the words of kindness that came from the Victim Support Counsellor who visited me the next morning. I remember her vividly: a messy, grey head of hair, thick glasses, a cigarette dangling from a crabbed hand as I opened my front door to let her in. Later, she would pat my knee with that hand kindly, lean forward, slide her glasses down her nose, look me dead in the eye, and say the most powerful thing anyone has ever said to me:

'You do know it wasn't your fault, don't you?'

I didn't know.

I had assumed it was my fault. But being told that it wasn't taught me something about kindness.

It taught me that for all the Bad Things that happen, Good Things also bloom.

I am fortunate to have lived a life thus far filled with many blessings. I try to concentrate on those as much as possible.

That being said, the Bad Things do still occasionally creep in through the cracks in the Good.

Hands where hands shouldn't go.

Crushing hangovers that couldn't be ascribed to alcohol alone.

Casual offers of flirting or sex mid-conversation from industry professionals.

Messages, pictures, looks, coercion, words, pinches, pokes, being pushed; push, push, push, all the time, always pushed. As a woman I find a large portion of my time is spent pushing back, and yes, it can become exhausting, and I find my bones ache with it, sometimes.

And as I move through life, and my career, and my body, and my hopes and dreams, I begin to notice these things happening to others around me. I notice victims speaking out, and I see the aftermath of that bravery. I see division and animosity and stress, I see polarisation and bickering and bullying and the absence of kindness, and I see silence, too. Dangerous silence. Complicit silence. Frightened silence. I see the wrong people dominating a discourse, I see ripples, nasty, cold ripples, spreading outwards from a dropped, dirty stone, and it infuriates me.

Thankfully, I am not alone. And that is where this Anthology germinated: from the seeds of discontent, fertilised by a resolve to act, to not remain silent, to do something positive.

To be a Good Thing, if at all possible.

And so we—myself, Laurel Hightower, and Cina Pelayo—have brought together this group of authors, this pack of wolves, to help us raise money for the survivors of harassment and abuse. The proceeds of our book will go to a selection of charitable organisations that offer direct support services to survivors; services that include information, advice, support, and therapy. We will continue to do this for as long as the first edition of the book remains in print, and hopefully, we might be able to take a Bad Thing, and turn it into the opposite, make our own ripples.

It goes without saying that this book does deal with some strong themes, themes that include descriptions of abuse, sexual abuse, harm to children, childbirth, bodily harm, self-harm, and child death, as well as more not explicitly listed here. We do therefore advise you to read with caution, even as we encourage you to engage with some of the themes and stories within, many of which are highly personal to the authors who wrote them.

Because we are not the sum of our damaged parts, we are not the Bad Things that happen to us, we are not the weariness we feel as we push, push, push. No, we are mothers, we are sisters, we are wives, daughters, partners, friends, lovers, survivors, victors, we are brilliant, shining things, but we are also the shadows at the end of the bed, the eyes that gleam in the dark, we are alpha, the things with teeth and claws and hearts of hot blood, and we stand side by fucking side, as a pack, and you can hear us singing, if you listen.

And we don't much care whether or not you like our song, because the time for that has long passed.

For we are wolves.

Gemma

THE BLACK WALLPAPER

Cynthia Pelayo

"I cry at nothing, and cry most of the time."—Charlotte Perkins Gilman, The Yellow Wallpaper

Eric and I rarely get away from the city. The city has its hold on us. Teeth clenched in the meat of our necks and sharp claws dug into our shoulders.

He had been asking for months, perhaps even years it seemed, for us to get away. I couldn't. First there was school. Then there was graduate school. Then there was work. And then, the blurred line between home life and work life blended into a watery existence where both became one.

I couldn't take time away from either because no matter where I turned there was someone coming to me with a request, a need for help, a chore, or just more work. Everything and everyone demanding more of me than I could ever provide. I was always needed. By someone. By something. And I was very tired.

"The Congress Plaza Hotel?" I questioned when we arrived.

"It's just for the night, and come on, you made vice president. We have to celebrate."

Being promoted to vice president had been such a long time coming, such a grueling process that I didn't even want to celebrate. I only wanted to sleep.

"We could have celebrated at home, with dinner…" I said.

"You mean you behind the glow of a laptop screen? People have to learn to live without you. We have our lives to live. Plus, I'd like kids someday, you know?"

I gave Eric a look that said not now. No one could live without me. On the drive here, my phone vibrated countless times. There were calls, voice messages, text messages, and alerts from various social media accounts. Everyone seemed to be looking for me.

"Don't answer," Eric said as he saw me reaching for my phone. "If there's any day anyone could wait, it's today. Hey," he said just as we parked the car and waited for the valet. "Any thoughts on the wallpaper in that room?"

I had many thoughts on the wallpaper in that room. I was happy, at least, that I was able to find a new wallpaper I liked for that room. The old wallpaper had been horrible. Yellow. I had never seen such horrible paper in my life.

"No," I answered. I didn't want to talk about the wallpaper. Not now at least. He laughed at me, and I ignored him.

"You were the one that wanted to change it."

I handed the valet the keys, and just as we reached the revolving doors of the hotel Eric sucked in some air through his front teeth, and stopped right before the doors. "I forgot my phone."

"Is the reservation under our name? I'll just check us in."

"You don't need to do that. You don't have to take care of everything and everyone." He was being especially nice and helpful. This was very unlike him.

"I'll check us in. Meet you at the bar?"

"Yes," he nodded, and I walked through the revolving

door, and then he was gone.

The reservation was in my name, and I laughed to myself because even in this small surprise gesture to do something nice for me, Eric felt the need to involve me at the planning stage.

"Just one night?" the woman at check-in asked.

"That's all I need," I answered.

I made a right, passing the large lobby, and moved toward the bar, which was so dated it now seemed modern in a weird way. Forced vintage. Visiting the bar at The Congress Plaza Hotel was an outing most Chicagoans had participated in at one point or another. Eric and I had visited the hotel's adjoining bar a few times in the past, to escape the biting cold after viewing New Year's Eve fireworks set across the sky at Navy Pier. It wasn't a premier or modern hotel, but it was a massive hotel, with historical significance situated along Michigan Avenue. It was old Chicago, and in many ways it represented me, us, our work ethic, and the hold this city held over us.

That's what we Chicagoans did: We worked hard. We endured time. And we did what sometimes seemed like the impossible. This hotel opened in 1893 and originally featured cobbled streets, gaslights and horse drawn carriages. I remembered that from when I was an undergraduate, working full-time and taking mostly afternoon and night classes so I could work during the day, paying my way through college. Most of my peers were on scholarships or their parents were paying for their schooling. I didn't have either luxury. One of my journalism professors worked as a walking tour guide, and one day she brought us out here to the hotel, to tell us about its structural and colorful history. I suppose this hotel had been a part of me for a very long time, and I suppose it would always be.

I took a seat at the bar. The bartender placed a cardboard coaster on the copper top counter in front of me. The image on the coaster was that of the hotel, two towers linked together by a smaller building in the center. I ordered an old-fashioned.

"Preference of whiskey?" He asked.

I once read that in an 1882 article from the Chicago Daily Tribune, a Chicago bartender said that the most popular of the in-vogue old-fashioned cocktails were made with whiskey. I looked at the shelf behind him.

"Death's Door," I said.

It seemed the fitting whiskey given the occasion and the place.

I placed my phone on the counter. My mother had called three times since I entered the hotel. My brother six. I had several new text messages, all of which I ignored. I wasn't going to read any of them. There was still no message from Eric. I turned to the photos in my phone and the first had been a collection of wallpaper swatches against the wall in that room.

"This paper looks vicious," I had said to myself when I was comparing patterns.

"How can paper look vicious?" Eric had asked.

"Some things have an influence on you," I answered.

That night Eric told me to go to sleep early, that he would help take care of things. Instead he fell asleep on the sofa. I stayed up all night preparing that room. The next day I lead five conference calls at work. Later that next night when I got home, I went to the basement where I kept my art supplies; acrylics and charcoals, canvas and pencils. I screamed because I wanted to paint but no longer knew how. Work, home, life had taken whatever creative energy I thought I had left.

My drink was ready and then it was gone. Another arrived. The sun outside had set, and the room filled. They were mostly tourists from out of town, surrounding suburbs, and nearby states who hated the city yet came here to play. A group of about twenty people stood just near the entrance of the bar, huddled around a figure with a curled mustache, dressed all in black.

"Sometimes, ladies and gentlemen," the man in black projected a radio announcer's voice that filled the bar "you will see that very light in the corner flicker."

The bartender noticed my look of curiosity. "Ghost tour," he said as he wiped the bar top with a white cloth. "Every Friday, Saturday, and Sunday."

I had done one of those tours before. A long time ago. It was just another thing that felt like the Chicago thing to do. The tour guide continued.

"There's very little connection to Al Capone and the hotel. The most I have been able to tie to him is that there are indications a phone call was made from the lobby of the hotel to his home in Florida just moments after the infamous St. Valentine's Day Massacre."

I glanced back at my phone. Now a call from my car dealership. I sighed. My car was more than overdue for an oil change. Yet another thing to do that I didn't have time for.

"You look tired," the bartender said.

"I am."

I had probably slept four hours that night before and probably less than that the night before that.

"Kids keeping you up late?"

"Everything's keeping me up late," I said.

"Did H.H. Holmes ever stay here?" a woman wearing a Chicago Cubs jersey asked a little too eagerly.

The bartender and I looked at each other and tried not to laugh. Tourists liked that about Chicago; they had an almost fervent need to know each and every gory detail of crimes from the past. Yet, crimes that occurred in the present repulsed them so that they flung hateful words about the city every time it made the news. Crimes of this city's past were once crimes of the present. Someone from the ghost tour group had motioned to the bartender and in minutes he was pouring beer into pint glasses.

"Before we make our way to the site of the Eastland Disaster at the Chicago River, three more horrifying things to note about this hotel."

The tour guide held out his left hand, holding up one finger. "First: The Florentine Room. There are tons of stories about whispers and phantom gunshots being heard from this ballroom when no one is there. One night a security guard quit on his first day when he heard music coming from this room, and no one was inside. Second: Another ballroom, the Gold Room. What I've mostly recorded about this room is a general feeling of unease. There have been accounts of people saying they heard a woman whisper into their ear. I can confirm that I experienced the same thing during one of my paranormal team's investigations."

"What does she say?" a teenage girl with blue-black hair asked.

"It's just this faint female whisper and it's difficult to make out what she's saying."

She's probably begging people to leave her alone, I thought.

"Finally, the Shadow Guy. Some people think it's the ghost of Captain Lou Ostheim, a Spanish–American War veteran who shot himself in the hotel in 1900 after waking up from a nightmare. A lot of guests have reported seeing this shadowy figure. One guard even told me that he chased it up to the rooftop, thinking it was a person before realizing what it was. There have been many other suicides here."

I tapped the glass on my phone. Still nothing from Eric. Once again I turned to the photos. I settled on the picture of the wallpaper I had chosen for that room.

"It has a sort of sub pattern," I remembered telling Eric as I held the paper to the light. "It's a different shade here, and here."

I pointed out the lace pattern within the paper, but he didn't look up once from his phone.

"Hey, my mom's having a birthday party for my dad tomorrow," he said. "Can you pick up a cake after work?"

"Really, Eric? You're telling me now? How many times have I told you I have a doctor's appointment tomorrow?"

His face was blank.

"I guess I'll take myself to the doctor."

That same day, I purchased a car, since I could no longer depend on him. My phone rattled on the counter.

"You're popular," the bartender said.

It was my mother calling again. She left a voice message I wouldn't check. Nearly every voice message I had in recent memory came from my mother. In nearly each message she ended with telling me I needed to sleep more, eat better, take care of myself. However, she never told me how.

I returned to the picture of the wallpaper. I remember how it looked like the first time I brought it into that room. The color. The embellishments. It's like that paper was made specifically for our house, and that room.

"Alright," the tour guide announced. "Make sure you settle up your tabs and let's be off."

A few members of the tour made their way back to the bar. The bartender printed up totals and handed out bills. The tour guide was a little more than a quarter way through with his beer when an older gentleman in a blue polo asked: "What about the sealed room?"

A few heads turned, seeking whatever gruesome find he could provide.

"I noticed there were a few young ones in the audience. I usually save that one for adult only shows, but," he searched nearby making sure there were no children in hearing distance. "None seem to be listening."

He knocked back the rest of his beer and set it on the counter.

"There's stories of a room being so haunted it had to be sealed off. Some say it was room 666, and actually, there really is an office where the number room 666 should be, but it's not numbered that, of course. There's also one other Chicago ghost tour guide, my old boss, who claims that Stephen King's '1408' is based off of a room here at the hotel, but that's not true. King never mentioned any specific room in this or any hotel in the introduction of '1408.'"

The old man shook his head. "No, that's not the one I'm thinking of."

The old man looked behind the tour guide and waved over to a woman in a bright peach blouse. She was holding a bag from the gift shop at the Art Institute of Chicago, multicolored scarves and art books peeking out from over the top of the bag.

"Dear, what was that one we were told about? On the thirteenth floor?"

I turned to the bartender and took another sip from my old-fashioned. He was scanning a credit card and shaking his head, again, trying not to laugh.

"No, it was the twelfth floor," the woman said.

The tour guide drew in a deep breath. "Yeah," he hesitated. The base of his radio announcer's voice faded. His participants now crowded around him, awaiting a tale he seemed hesitant to share.

"The Congress Plaza used to house immigrants and refugees from around World War II. In 1939, forty-three-year-old Adele Langer of Czech-Jewish descent had been staying at the hotel with her two sons, Jan Misha and Karel Tommy. Her husband wasn't there, since his travels had been delayed. Adele and her children were in the country on a six-month visa, which was scheduled to expire. Adele grew nervous. Her husband wasn't there. The threat of deportation hung over her. She was in a foreign country with her two small children, and she was alone. She grew depressed. Worried. Overwhelmed. On August 4th of that year, she took her children to the zoo for the day. They returned to their room on the twelfth floor. There, she called her children over to a window. She opened it. She pushed them both out. Then, she jumped out of the window herself. What's worse is right after their deaths, an unopened letter was found awaiting the family's response. They had been offered permanent refugee status in Canada."

"Maybe that's the horrible sealed off room people talk about," the woman said. The tour guide agreed and then rushed his group off to their next destination. To another location of murder and mayhem. This city was host to many.

My phone vibrated. The blue screen alerting.

"I'm at the room. Where are you?"

I rolled my eyes and silently cursed Eric. Like always he had completely ignored or just entirely forgotten what I had said.

"Told you I'd meet you at the bar."

"Sorry. Coming."

"No, Fine. Wait there," I responded.

After walking past the lobby, going to the gilded elevator and down a long corridor, I met Eric in our room on the eleventh floor. The front desk had given him a keycard. He was seated on the bed. The room was furnished no worse than inharmonious.

"Welcome to a Lakeview King Room." He took my bag and set it down. "Where you have a king-sized bed, decorative round table, two chairs, and a desk where I hope you will not be working from all night."

"Where'd the valet park the car?" I removed my jacket and hung it in the closet. "Back at our house?"

"The car was blocked in. An accident or something. Didn't you hear the sirens?"

"No," I sat down on the bed and allowed myself to fall back against the stiff mattress. My entire body ached. "I'm so tired."

"You work too hard."

"You say that like I have a choice. I have to work. There's the house, and every single repair that seems to come up at the most inconvenient time. My student loans. My credit card debt. My car. My mom's car…"

"I know you like taking care of them…"

"Like taking care of them? I have to take care of them. If I let my brothers take care of them both my blind father and diabetic mother would be near death."

"I'm sorry," he said. "Maybe you should go back to painting. You were happier when you were painting."

I laughed.

"Find me the time to paint."

I was so mad I wanted to cry, but I didn't. I had learned to hold it in until it burned. I lay my arm across my eyes. That did a decent job of blocking out the light. The lighting in the room was that dim.

"How was the bar?"

"Fine. Old-fashioneds and entertainment."

I moved my arm away and sat up. "Dammit." I remembered an email I owed my boss.

"Entertainment?"

I dug my laptop out of my bag and lay it on the desk. "Some ghost tour came into the lobby and then the bar. Don't you remember? We did one of those, geez, ages ago. I think we were still dating."

"I don't remember," he said.

Eric had selective memory. He only remembered what he wanted to.

"Don't you remember? We did one with my brother and that one girlfriend of his."

"Sorry," he shrugged. "Anything interesting you hear from the tour?"

"Just classic Chicago hauntings, and thank goodness we're not staying on the twelfth floor," I said, "because there's some godawful room that's sealed off."

"Do you hear that?" he asked.

"No." I was typing away at my keyboard, and my phone continued to vibrate. "I can't believe I forgot about this stupid project they assigned me to. Like I don't already have a ton of projects at work. How am I supposed to get any of this done? When am I supposed to sleep? Eat? Live? It's ridiculous."

"It's getting louder." Eric stood up, and at the window he pulled back the curtains. The room faced a brick wall. "Still more sirens," he said.

"It's Friday night in Chicago. What'd you expect?"

I yawned and then looked at myself in the mirror. Exhaustion made it so that I no longer recognized myself.

"How many hours of sleep did you get last night?"

"Barely four. My fitness tracker told me that this morning."

"I never thanked you," he said. "For putting up that wallpaper. I know I should have done it…"

"It's up. It doesn't matter anymore."

"What do you think? Are you happy with it? It's black wallpaper."

There were things in that wallpaper nobody but me knew, or would ever know.

"It's wallpaper." I hit send on the email and exhaled. "I think I actually have a few minutes to breathe."

"I got you a present," he said.

Eric never got me presents. Valentine's Day. Anniversaries. Never. He said 'what was the point' when we got things for each other all of the time. By things I think he meant that huge house we bought that I wound up rehabbing by myself.

"I got you a few of those fizzy bath things from that place you love so much," he dangled the bag in front of my face. I looked inside.

"Lavender bath bombs. Wow. It's like you're forcing me to relax."

I wish he had done this before, things like this. It would have made things much better if he had helped. Things could have been different.

"Yes, and I'm serious. You do too much. You really need to relax."

I couldn't relax. Not now. Not ever.

"Who's going to live my life if I don't live it?"

I felt a sting behind my eyes. I blinked back tears. I wasn't going to allow myself to cry.

"It's okay if you can't do everything. Work can wait. Your parents. The house. Maybe you just need to focus on you for a little bit."

My phone continued vibrating. "I can't deal with this anymore."

"Just turn it off."

For the first time in a long time I did just that. I reached for my phone and I turned it off. I put it in my bag and promised to never look at it again.

"Are you okay?" he asked.

"It's just…fine. I'll be fine," I lied. "I got promoted. I should be happy, but how long did I have to wait to get promoted? There are people ten, fifteen years younger than me that have made vice president, that are better daughters, sisters, wives, freelance artists, mothers…"

"You can be all of those things," Eric said.

I thought of that undulating wallpaper in the moonlight and how alone I felt. How physically exhausted and in pain I felt. I was none of those things that Eric said, and I would never be. No matter how hard I worked. No matter what I did, I was not as successful as I needed to be, wanted to be. I was not enough for everything I needed to do. "I have a studio in the basement I haven't touched since we bought the house."

"But the wallpaper…"

"The wallpaper stains everything it touches. My clothes are stained. My hands. I'll never be the same, because I can't sleep."

I stood up and felt my body scream in pain.

"I'm just mad. I thought I'd have more right now. I'd have more together, and I feel like nothing's good enough. Like I'm not enough. No matter how hard I work. No matter what I do. I'll never be good enough, and I'm just so tired, and sleep's just getting in the way of me doing all that I need to do…Shit…"

"What?" he asked.

"Did we lock the doors to the house?"

"I don't think that matters right now," he said.

My computer pinged.

"Don't answer it. Your boss can wait. Go, take a bath," he opened the door to the bathroom. "This is your time to finally relax."

In the bathroom, I started the water in the bathtub. I set the temperature as hot as would be tolerable. My body ached. My head, arms, shoulders, hips, feet, everything ached this intense heavy ache as if my body had been taken apart and put back together, but just slightly off.

"You sure you don't hear that? That noise. It's driving

me nuts."

Eric shouted from the other room. "I'm sure it'll stop soon."

When the water reached a comfortable level, I dropped the bath bomb in the water. The packed ball of Epsom salt, essential oil of lavender and light purple coloring fizzed, making this silent, soft hiss. I took my clothes off and set them on top of the shelf. Beside the tub I set my toiletry bag. My feet touched the water and it was hot, but satisfactory. I allowed my body to sink into the tub. My muscles tensed. It was as if I was physically incapable of relaxing. Even surrounded by steaming hot water in calming oils, every fiber within me refused to be at ease.

"Tell me about that sealed-off room? What's so horrible about it?"

"Some mother went mad. Pushed her children out the window and then committed suicide. She was alone. Depressed. No one seemed to help her when she needed help the most."

"What do you think about kids?" Eric asked just outside the door.

"I think that I'll be the one taking care of them, just like I take care of everything else and everyone else. Plus, I barely sleep now. I'll never sleep."

"You act like I don't help out."

"You do, sometimes. I mean…" I splashed some water on my face. "I just don't know. How can we be parents? We just bought that house."

"The house is huge. That room is perfect for kids."

"When will I ever sleep?"

"We'll take turns," he said.

I laughed. I laughed so hard I knew it hurt him. I wanted to hurt him. "Take turns? You say that, but that's not what you did. Did you?"

He didn't answer my question.

"Do you hear the sirens?"

His voice sounded distant, but I heard the sirens now, and they were loud.

"Eric, are they getting closer?"

He remained silent. Maybe he had fallen asleep. Just like Eric, to tell me that he cared, that he would help, just like he told me he would help with the wallpaper and he didn't. I put up the wallpaper in the nursery all by myself. When we brought the baby home, I'm the one who stayed up all night with the baby, feeding and changing. I was the one who would go to work all day on four hours of sleep, or less, and do it all over again, feeding and changing, and then there was the wallpaper. I was tired. I was angry. I was in pain.

That pattern haunted me.

When I tried to pull the wallpaper off and it wouldn't break away, that's when I laid the baby down in its crib, went downstairs, and got a lighter.

There was a pound on the door to the room.

I sat up straight in the bathtub.

"Eric, did you hear that?" I reached for a towel, but I knew it was too late. I remained in the tub.

"Do you smell that?" I heard him ask.

I did. It smelled like something burning. In the next room a baby wailed. There was another series of knocks at the door. Pounding. This time more urgent.

"Eric," I whispered, but I knew he wasn't there.

There were more knocks at the door, as if two or more

people were banging on the surface, trying to break in. Then a man's voice outside the door called my name.

"If you don't open the door we're coming in!"

I heard the crackle of a walkie-talkie just outside.

"Yeah, she's holed up in a hotel room. We'll get her out."

I reached for my toiletry bag and leaned back against the tub. I removed the straight razor blade from its casing. There was another series of pounds. A warning that they had a keycard and would be entering. They called my name, and said I would be arrested. They called my name again. Always my name being called. Always someone looking for me to do something for them. Eric and this hotel. This hotel and this city. This city and me. All part of some tragedy. Some great Chicago fire.

I drew the blade first across my right wrist, digging deep into the thin flesh, feeling the tiny bones snap. Then I felt the pop of my veins as I submerged my hand under the water. A spray of red. I repeated this to my left wrist and closed my eyes. I listened as the baby cried. I listened to the sirens that awaited me not only outside of the hotel room, but which were now approaching my house. Now engulfed in flames. My husband asleep on the sofa in front of the TV, ten sleeping pills I slipped into his afternoon coffee. The black wallpaper in the nursery, burning blacker and curling back on itself. The baby, just weeks old, screaming in its crib for me, everybody screaming for me, always needing me to do something for them, screaming for me…

Originally published in She's Lost Control, 2019

THOUGH YOUR HEART IS BREAKING

Laurel Hightower

Sarah stared down at the blood, dried and crusted on her hands. It had woven itself into the smallest creases of her palms, and she had a memory, fleeting, of how they'd looked when the blood was fresh. Like shiny leather gloves, elbow length. The kind of thing she might have worn to prom, back when she'd been young.

Now the blood had faded, cracked. It was peeling and flaking away whenever she moved, and she could tell it was driving the officer crazy, the one who was standing in the corner, watching her. Babysitting her until the grown-ups returned, with more questions Sarah didn't know how to answer. The strongest images in her mind were of her blood gloved hands and snatches of a song, one she couldn't quite name.

She turned her hands over and stared at the teeth marks embedded deep in all four fingers of each hand. She frowned at them, still trying to discern what they meant. Because the odd thing was, the marks were only on the inside of her hands. Nothing marred the flesh of the outside, except dried blood.

***

Helena stared at the body, one hand cupping the other elbow, her free palm across her mouth. Dark eyebrows bunched. Lips tight. Thinking.

"That is, hands down, the grossest thing I've ever seen."

She glanced at Max, but he didn't look like he was going to toss his cookies. He was bent close to the dead man's neck, trying to get a visual on the inside of the throat. He'd thought there might be something in there, *Silence-of-the-Lambs*-style. It wasn't a bad thought, and Helena marked another point in the invisible score book she kept for all new partners.

"It reminds me of something," she said, walking another slow circle around the kitchen chair where the dead man slumped.

Max straightened, shook his head. "No way. Nothing like this has *ever* come across. I'd know—I'd remember something like that."

Max was young, early thirties, and the newest detective on Helena's squad, but he'd spent years studying and organizing the evidence archives, looking at all the open, and closed, cases that had passed through over the years.

She shook her head. "I don't think it was a case...something else. I can't quite..."

Taylor Eckles snapped another photo, standing on a step stool and aiming down into the exposed airway. "Looks almost like a weird kinda fuckin' muppet, the way his face is spread like that."

Max shot her a look, but Helena snapped her fingers. "*Beetlejuice.* That's what it reminds me of."

Max moved to her shoulder, craned his head. "That old movie with the crazy Baldwin dude? I don't see it."

"It was one of the scenes after they cross to the other

31

side, when they're trying to scare the family. Geena Davis's head's all stretched out, her eyes are in her mouth? That's kinda what this looks like."

Max frowned, fished his phone out, and a short search later was giving her a hesitant hand waggle. "I guess so. The way the teeth are, maybe."

The victim, thirty-seven-year-old Brock Kirkland, had his upper and lower jaw broken. They'd been snapped back so far it was like someone had crammed their hands down his throat and pulled in opposite directions. The result was a head broken nearly in half, starting at the guy's mouth. The halves lay open, teeth exposed on either side, and a direct view down the guy's gullet. Torn skin hung in flaps where his cheeks had once been. Helena thought she could even make out the flaccid remains of a dimple, before deciding she should probably stop looking at it.

"Ready to head back?" asked Max when she turned her back on the corpse. There was more than a little relief in his voice.

She sighed. "I guess. I still don't think it was her."

He scrunched his mouth to one side. "You just don't want it to be her."

"C'mon, Maxie, you see that little thing having the upper body strength to rip that guy's face in half?"

He shrugged. "Maybe she used something, an instrument of some kind. She could've—"

Helena scowled. "Who the fuck is humming that song? It's driving me crazy."

Max raised an eyebrow. "I don't hear anything. What song is it?"

She listened, but it was gone. "Fuck if I know.

Something old, I think." She raised a finger. "Refrain from making the obvious jokes, please."

Max sniffed. "I *never* make obvious jokes. Can we go back now?"

Helena tossed her gloves and booties into the waiting evidence bag. "Yeah. I've got more questions."

***

Helena grabbed a bottled water and a couple pieces of dark chocolate from the stash at her desk. She tapped on the door, and Randy Bellows, the cop she'd put on babysitting duty, squeezed past her on his way out the door. She glowered and stood her ground.

"Sorry, ma'am. Close quarters." He grinned down at her, and she crossed her arms, shoved into his space.

"I don't give a fuck how close the quarters are. You brush my tits like that again, you're gonna lose a hand."

"Sorry, ma'am." He wasn't and didn't care if she knew it. He would before too long.

Bellows leaned against the wall instead of fucking off like he should have. "That's an odd bird in there."

She didn't ask him to elaborate. Usually she appreciated observations from her team, but Randy Bellows wasn't on her team, he just wanted to be.

He didn't take the hint, looking back over his shoulder through the one-way glass. "I still can't picture how she overpowered him, a big guy like that." He waited, but when she didn't answer, he finally pushed off the wall. "Anyway, hope you got some more insight on your little field trip, and didn't just go for Chinese." He smirked, clapped Max on the shoulder and kept walking.

Max watching dispassionately. "I'm sure he thinks that's hilarious."

"I'm sure he does."

"Do you think he knows I'm Korean, and he's trying to be a prick, or does he actually think all Asians come from China?"

"I'm not in his head, Max. Thank Christ. You coming?"

He shuffled into the room behind her, and Helena sat across from the blood-covered woman. She opened the bottle of water and pushed it across the table, then followed it up with the chocolate.

Sarah stared down at the foil wrapped pieces and smiled. "Thank you."

"You're welcome. You want to wash your hands first?"

The other woman shook her head. "I don't think so. I'm trying to...remember." She held her hands out in front of her, frowning at them.

Helena sat back, avoided Max's eyes. "You don't remember what happened?"

"Not...exactly, no. I saw the body, though. I know what it looks like." She raised her hands. "What this looks like."

Helena nodded. "So, you understand why you're here, then."

Sarah smiled again, a small amount of color returning to her pallid face. "I do."

"So why don't you start with how you knew the victim?"

She frowned; eyebrows drawn down. "I don't know who—oh. You mean him."

"Right. Brock Kirkland. How'd you know him?"

Sarah shook her head. "Oh, I didn't. Not at all."

Helena frowned. "Then how did he come to be in your home?"

The woman's eyes slid to the side; her lips parted. "I...well, I believe I asked him in."

Helena's eyes flicked to Max's face, but he was frowning, concentrating on Sarah. No smirk or judgment. Good. Give the kid another invisible star.

"And did you ask him in for...romantic purposes?"

Sarah laughed. "Sex, you mean? No, I didn't, but it may have been what he thought."

Helena leaned forward. "Was he coming on to you? A sexual assault?"

Max coughed—leading, she knew she was doing it. But she wanted to understand. And yeah, she wanted the circumstances to be mitigating. There was something calm and a little broken about the woman sitting in front of her. But there was also something strong and shining, that Helena felt herself responding to.

The other woman shook her head, looked into her lap. "It wasn't like that."

Helena had never been good at waiting, but she tried, giving the suspect space. Finally, Sarah lifted her head.

"Do you remember, Detective, the absolute worst time someone told you to smile?"

Her breath caught in her chest. She did, actually, with vivid clarity. She didn't need to look at Max to know he was confused, but it wasn't a thing men dealt with.

The woman was waiting for a response.

"I do," she said, and left it at that. It wasn't a memory she wanted to recount. Standing in line at a Dollar

General, a pack of maxi pads in one hand, feeling the hope slide down her leg. She'd been nine days late after three years of trying for the baby she'd wanted for so long. It wasn't enough. She'd barely been holding herself together, then she heard the man behind her in line whisper loudly to his girlfriend.

"Would it kill her to smile? Jesus, like I want to look at a face like that."

If she hadn't been so hollow inside, Helena might have socked him; punched him in the dick and asked him why he wasn't smiling through the pain. But the hurt of the other was too near, too heavy, so she'd just paid for her pads and gone home to cry.

She didn't say any of that here, now, because the grief of that time in her life was still too close, even a decade later. There'd never been a baby, and now there never would be. But even though she didn't say it, she felt like Sarah read it on her. The other woman reached out with her blood-covered hand before stopping herself.

"I can see you do. I can, too. A lot of us do. You want to hear mine?"

Helena nodded.

Sarah turned to watch her own reflection in the glass. "I was leaving my doctor's office. I was twenty-two, and I'd just gone to be tested for STDs, after being sexually assaulted."

Max made a sharp movement in his forgotten corner, but neither of the women looked at him.

"I was clean, but they told me I'd have to wait and be retested for HIV. I'd locked my keys in my car and had to call Pop-a-Lock. The guy, when he showed up, was all smiles and flirting. It was like he had no idea where we were. And it was all I could do to respond, to even hear him when he spoke. I was dying on the inside, and he didn't even notice. Then when he was leaving, he told me to smile." Her bloody hands clenched together on the tabletop, and Helena watched flakes crunch up and drift away.

"That's fucked up," said Max.

Sarah turned to look at him, offered another smile. "It really is, isn't it?"

"Was that him? Tonight, the guy? Was he the one that told you that? Is that why?"

Helena sat forward, frowned at him.

"No," said Sarah, turning to face forward again. "No, that was decades ago. I still remember, though."

"So, what, then?" asked Helena. "What's the connection?"

Sarah shrugged. "The connection is simple. He said it to me, tonight. I was walking home from the bus stop. It was cold, and I've been sick for a week. I was thinking about all the papers I had to grade, and the fact that I'll have to move my mom into assisted living soon. She's going to fight me on it, and I don't blame her. He was leaving a convenience store, the one on the corner of Vine and Market?"

Helena nodded. She knew the one.

"And he just glanced at me and told me to smile, it wasn't that bad." Her pale face scrunched up. "But it *was*? You know? It was."

"Yeah," Helena replied, her voice soft.

"So, I asked him to step up to my place. It was close, less than a block. I'm sure he thought he was about to get lucky, so he did. And then, when we got inside, I just..."

Her voice faded; she dropped her gaze to her lap again.

Helena cleared her throat. "How?"

Sarah's brow wrinkled. "That's what I've been trying to remember. I've been looking at my hands and thinking of ways I must have done it. But...I can't see it."

"What do you see?"

Sarah looked up, past Helena to the room's stark ceiling. "What is that? What's that song? I keep thinking I remember the name, the lyrics, but every time I try..."

"Sarah. What do you see?"

Her gaze found Helena's again. "I don't *see* anything. That's the trouble. It's what I hear. Like the psychic scream of every woman who's been told to smile through the pain. Not because it'll make things better for her, you know? But so her *face* doesn't bother the people around her."

Helena frowned, watching her. Because for a moment it was as though she heard that scream as well. Not here, not now, but ten years ago, feeling hope slide out of her in thick, dark gouts.

She stood, pushed away from the table. "We'll be back. Sit tight."

Sarah didn't seem to notice, staring at the ceiling again.

Max followed her out and to the break room for coffee. He poured hers black, into the mug she liked. She went to the window and looked out into the night, smeared by too bright lights.

He moved to her shoulder, but not too close. Max was good with space bubbles.

"Pretty fucked up," he said.

"Which part?"

38

"All of it. What that guy said to her, back then. Right after...you know. And then tonight..." he cleared his throat. "Do you think it's...I mean, is it always that bad? Like, enough to kill for?"

Helena thought about it. Seeing her own reflection transposed across the dark, dirty night. "No. Most of the time it isn't. It's annoying and condescending. Like the guy telling me to smile while I'm working out. Fuck off, right? I'm benching 160, so spot me or move on. But sometimes it hurts. Sometimes it's the last thing you need, and it's piled on top of a whole lot of other psychic baggage. The way our bodies are seen as out there for public consumption, commentary. Right down to the expression on our faces."

Max sipped his coffee. "I never thought about it that way. I always thought it was a douchey thing to do, but think of saying that to somebody on the worst day of their lives."

"Yeah." She frowned, tilted her head. "Tell me you hear that."

Max looked around. "The humming? Yeah, I think it's her." He jerked his head in the direction of Interview One, only a wall away from where they stood.

"You know the song?"

He frowned. "No, I can't quite...but it does seem familiar." He snapped his fingers.

"This turning into *West Side Story*?" snarked Bellows, edging in to get to the coffee. They both ignored him.

Phones began to ring, all over the station. Dispatch lit up with a hundred calls, but Helena was hearing something else. A cry, of a hundred thousand voices at once. She winced, dropped her coffee, and slapped her hands to her head as the scream shivved into her frontal lobe. She saw a thousand faces, unsmiling, unhappy, hurting. Felt their hearts breaking as one.

Max was at her shoulder, saying something, asking what was wrong.

Bellows leaned against the table. "Smile, boss. It's not that bad."

The scream stopped. The pain went with it, but then another scream started. This one from deep in Bellows's throat. Helena watched, fascinated, as his eyes rolled back in his head, his mouth stretching impossibly wide. The skin strained, pulled tight. A nauseating crack as both jaws broke at once, and the man's face split from his lips back to his ears. The top of his head flipped open, like a mangled Venus flytrap. His scream tapered off into a gargle, then even that went silent as he slid to the floor.

"Jesus," said Max, retching beside her. "Jesus, what the fuck—"

The phones were still ringing. Screams in the street below, but above it all, Helena could hear singing. Maybe it was Sarah, or maybe it was only in her head, but it was a relief to recognize the song at last.

She looked into Bellows's esophagus, spurting blood, and wondered if he was finding life worthwhile.

ANGEL

Gemma Amor

"Can I help you?" Sylvia Thorne said, and with those four words, Angel made a split-second judgement about the other woman: she hated her, right then and there on the spot.

She kept this to herself, though. Neutrality was armor, and she had hers burnished bright.

The woman, Sylvia, glanced back over her shoulder at the barbeque she'd begrudgingly left in her backyard. It looked like a good party from what Angel could see, a July 4th cookout. There were people everywhere, eating, drinking, laughing. Someone had rigged up a sprinkler, and small slippery kids in bright swimsuits were hopping in and out of it, shrieking with joy. Bright sunlight shone through the water spray. Angel saw shimmering rainbows explode as the children burst through them, only to re-form, iridescent droplets hanging like jewels in the air: nature's chandelier. She saw exposed bellies, tattoos, red skin, long, lean legs and short, hairy legs, and bare feet, and shiny, sunburned faces, getting darker and redder as alcohol began to marinade the flesh. She saw smoke, smelled chicken and burgers on a grill, heard music playing loud and brash from a duo of speakers laid out on the thirsty grass.

She saw longing in the woman in front of her. The suspect wanted to get back to the party as quickly as possible.

Angel was about to fuck that idea up real hard.

Such a shame.

"Are you Sylvia Thorne?" She asked, and then waited for it to happen, feeling weary to her core. The tall woman with broad shoulders and strong arms and a rash of adult acne across her chin looked Angel up and down from the safety of her doorway. Specifically, she absorbed the color of Angel's skin, which was obviously a shade or two less than pure white for Sylvia's tastes. On noticing this, Sylvia's lip curled.

There it is, Angel thought.

The suspect swelled up like a puffer fish, then, sharp, vicious *'fuck-off'* spines virtually popping out all over her body, one by one, *pop, pop, pop goes the racist!*

Until, as they always did, she registered Angel's partner, Officer Salt, all six-foot-Caucasian-male-five of him. He was a blondie, to boot, with a crew cut hairstyle that could only be described as Kurt-Russell-chic. He looked like a poster boy for people like Sylvia, but he wouldn't have been happy about that had you told him. He and Angel were tight, they worked well together and had the kind of relationship that two people who see the kinds of things they see, day in, day out, have. He chewed on a wad of gum with his head held back, squinting down his nose at Sylvia with naked dislike, and she slowly and very visibly sucked her spines back in, one by one.

Angel sighed.

"Ma'am?" she said, dragging Sylvia's attention back, moving her head so the woman was forced to make a visual connection with her. "Can you answer the question? Are you Sylvia Thorne?"

The other woman nodded, reluctantly.

"You police?"

It was an inane question, because the uniforms made it pretty fucking obvious that they were police.

"What's this about, Officer?"

Green eyes bored into Angel, and they would have been pretty if they'd had any hint of kindness in them, or was Angel projecting too much? Probably. The woman's tone was strangely pleasant now, it had switched lighting fast to something more polite, the kind of voice that answered calls in an office, all business efficiency and good manners, hot butter wouldn't melt. Angel's dislike of the suspect swelled, doubled in size, threatened to stick in her craw, but she knew she was being unprofessional, she knew she had to keep a lid on it, so she stuck to the script, as hard as that was.

"Ma'am," she said, maintaining steady eye contact without giving anything of herself away. "We've received a call that a child in this house is currently in danger." She delivered this as calmly as she knew how, as if it was no big deal, as if she was talking about the weather or the price of beer. It was taking every inch of her resolve, however, to not pull her weapon and kick Sylvia out of the way to search the house, but she knew that would be detrimental to the cause—this situation had to be handled as carefully as possible. She didn't want to give the sack of shit before her a single loophole to wriggle through when she ended up in court, and so Angel was going to do everything by the book, even if she hated the fucking book with a passion born of bitter experience.

"Think we can come inside and talk about this a little more?" Angel said, and next to her, Salt rolled his head around on his neck, loosening himself up, subconsciously

43

preparing for a hustle. Angel heard a joint pop as he did so, and it made her think of the meat cooking out on the grill in the yard, the smell of which permeated the air so heavily it made her queasy. Who wanted to eat in heat like this anyway? A bead of sweat rolled down the side of her face; she ignored it.

Sylvia blinked, but that was the extent of her emotional reaction. A brief closing of her eyelids, a momentary respite in focus, as if she were a lizard on a rock. A lizard was a good way to describe Sylvia. There was something scaly and reptilian about her. Something unfathomably cold.

"A call from who?" The woman said, eventually, those lizard eyes wide and direct, and Angel knew then that her suspicions were well on the way to being confirmed. Sylvia didn't ask which one of her five children was supposedly at risk. She didn't go pale, or look worried, or scared, or confused, or angry. She didn't act like a mother who had just been told one of her babies was in danger. She acted like someone thinking fast, someone coming up with their own script, a script that minimized the damage to their own self, and people only wrote new internal narratives like that on the fly when they had something to hide.

"From a resident of this household," Angel said, noncommittally. She let that sink in for a moment, saw shock and then fury race across the woman's features before she smoothed them away.

Angel couldn't tell her that the call had come in an hour ago from Sylvia's own nine-year-old daughter, a girl who refused to give anyone her name.

"My baby sister's dyin'," the girl had said down the

phone. She was crying so hard no one could understand her, at first. "She's dyin', and Mom won't do nothing about it."

The call operator who spoke to the frightened child had burst into tears immediately after hanging up and had been sent home for the day to recover. Angel remembered the deep hush that had settled on herself and Salt when dispatch had radioed through with orders to get out there as soon as possible and investigate the claim.

Just stick to the script, she told herself. *You owe this person nothing.*

Salt, happy to let Angel drive until now, took a step forward. He was as conscious of time slipping away, and less caring of the rulebook. "Ma'am," he said, and his voice had more of an obvious effect on Sylvia than Angel's because she flinched and took a half-step back inside.

"State law says that if we have reasonable suspicion of someone in your home being under threat or in danger of their life, particularly a minor, then we're allowed to come inside with, or without your cooperation, so I'd suggest doing this the easy way, not the hard."

Sylvia was still thinking, licking her lips as she worked through several different scenarios in her brain. There was a small smudge of something like barbeque sauce on the corner of her mouth. Her tongue found it, worried at it whilst Angel watched, half-fascinated, half-repulsed.

"Don't you need a warrant?" Sylvia said, eventually.

"Not in this case, Ma'am," Angel said, and her hand went to her hip where her gun was holstered. She made the action deliberately, and Sylvia registered it, understood what it meant. Realizing she was in a corner, the tall woman took a final, sad look at the barbeque over her shoulder, and stepped out of the way, shrugging as she did so. Sylvia had her own armor, and its fabric was nonchalance.

"I think this is all a lot of fuss over nothing," she said, and later, Angel would remember the look on her face as she said that, she would remember how innocent Sylvia thought she sounded.

Back in this moment, Angel stared at Sylvia warily as she entered the house, then cleared her throat.

"You have a child here called Leila?" She asked, another formality, for she already knew the answer.

"My baby, yes," Sylvia replied.

Angel felt a quiet fury building inside of her.

"The call we received was about the wellbeing and safety of Leila. She's eleven months old, right?"

Sylvia nodded.

"Ma'am, may we see her?"

Sylvia said nothing, only stood, thinking, the cogs in her head working overtime. Salt grew impatient, folded his arms.

"It's not really a request," he grumbled, and Sylvia shook her head, then, and turned wordlessly, knowing her number was up, understanding that her dirty little secrets weren't about to be so secret any more.

She beckoned for the officers to follow and led them down a narrow corridor to Leila's room. It was easy enough to single out, because someone, another child, maybe the same child that had placed the call to 911, had shakily drawn the name on the outside of the bedroom door in blue crayon, only they had spelled it wrong, so it said 'LAYLA,' and that tiny detail, that tiny little spelling mistake, so innocuous and well-meaning, would stay with both police officers for a long, long time, haunting their dreams in lurid, scribbled blue.

***

At first, Angel mistook Leila for a doll, she was so tiny. She was expecting an infant girl with the proportions of an eleven month old toddler, but the child they found, lying on her back in a near comatose state on a dirty, stinking, urine-soaked mattress spotted with brown stains and black, speckled toxic mold, couldn't have weighed more than eight or nine pounds at most: no more than a newborn. The sheer state of her extreme malnourishment sent a wave of ice cold shock through Angel's body, a rushing, roaring tsunami of bewilderment, a feeling of such ferocity that she realized she'd never experienced real, true horror until that moment in her life, until she saw the shallow rise and fall of Leila's chest, until she heard the dry rattle of the child's breath, until she felt her weak, stuttering pulse, touched her cold, rough, scaly skin, and smelled the stink of her days-old, unchanged, over-full, leaking, filthy diaper.

And she knew, without question, that the child was dying. Dying of neglect, dying of hunger and dehydration while unsuspecting partygoers gorged themselves on charcoaled meat and icy sodas not more than twenty feet away.

Angel covered her mouth, gagging at the overwhelming stench of urine and feces and mold and neglect that seemed to fill every single inch of space around her. Salt let fly a strangled curse word: "Fuck," he said, then, "*Fuck*. The fuck is this?!" His hands trembled as they went to his radio to call for assistance.

Angel's vision turned inwards, retreated into a blooming, escapist fantasy. She lost sight of the terrible scene in front of her, lost sight of the tiny, twiggy legs and bony arms and sunken, graying face of the ragdoll infant who lay gasping her last in her dirty cot. Instead, she imagined a different version of the child, plump, pink, lively, with sparkling eyes and glossy hair and dimples and pillowy rolls of fat in all the right places.

Behind all this, snippets of conversation faded in and out of Angel's earshot, as if carried on an indecisive wind. Salt asking for backup. Ambulance sirens in the distance. A different voice asking Sylvia "When did this child last eat?" In horrified, choked tones.

Sylvia refused to answer. She was clever enough not to incriminate herself any further with any half-baked excuses or open, unsubstantiated lies. That tongue of hers kept flickering out of her mouth though, wetting her bottom lip, her only visible sign of anxiety. A lizard basking on a rock, cold blood pumping sluggishly in her veins.

Leila coughed, weakly, and Angel snapped out of her fantasy as instantly as she'd sunk into it. She stared down at the baby girl and tried desperately to understand what she should be doing to help. She tried to recall her medical training, but as far as she could remember, it had not dealt with how to treat extreme starvation. She dithered, too afraid to touch Leila, too afraid that even the most gentle of interferences would spell death for the infant. She desperately wanted to rip off the disgusting diaper and pour water into the child's mouth, find a food pouch, jam in as much food as quickly as she could, but she was frightened, frightened of making it worse, and so she just stood there. She couldn't even cover the shivering girl with a blanket, there were none. She briefly considered ripping the curtains off the rail over the window, but upon seeing how stained and filthy they were, decided against it.

Eventually, as Salt continued to question Sylvia with a mounting, seething fury—he was a father of four, all of them girls—Angel sank down quietly to her knees beside the cot, and delicately threaded her hand through the bars surrounding the child, resting her index finger lightly, so lightly, upon the tiny, cold palm closest to her. The small fingers twitched, but Leila was too weak to take a proper hold of Angel's finger.

"It's okay, baby," Angel whispered, and she hoped the child could at least hear her, could absorb some of her warmth through her finger, through the simple act of being touched, and, maybe, by proxy, some of her love, because if anyone needed love, it was Leila.

And Angel had love to give.

She sat like that until the ambulance came, prayers slipping from her mouth like spilled beads, and later, Salt would have to forcibly drag her away from the cot so the paramedics could work on the child. Ultimately, it would be for nothing, because Leila had already left that wretched place, her soul halfway to the stars, while Angel, in a great act of disservice to her own name, remained tethered to the earth, her skin too heavy to allow her to fly.

***

Angel went home later that night and lit a candle. Salt offered to come inside, give her some company, but she didn't want company. She wanted to be alone. Other people were like clashing cymbals to her right now: too demanding of her attention, too jarring in their presence.

Salt, however, wasn't taking no for an answer. He had seen a queer look in her eye when they had received confirmation of Leila's death. A queer, stricken look that went beyond the tragedy of the situation they'd found themselves in.

And he had a fairly good idea what it was that she was struggling with.

"I'd rather be by myself right now," Angel said, softly, and Salt nodded. "I know you would. But I'd rather know you're okay, first. So I'm coming in, whether you like it or not."

Angel relented, silently unlocking her door. Her colleague followed her inside, made her sit on the couch while he uncorked a bottle of red wine, moving with familiarity around her home.

She wondered, as she sat there, about the woman, Sylvia. She wondered how someone could be so undeserving of the gift she had been given—a child, a beautiful child. She wondered how someone could regard a human life so poorly as to decide to not feed, to not clean, to not nourish, to not love. She wondered about that last thing the most. How could a mother decide not to love? How did that become a conscious choice, like switching off running water from a tap? Angel went over it again and again and again, but could come up with no answers. People did bad things to other people, she knew this, she had worked in law enforcement long enough to see evidence of that firsthand, but the crimes that had, until today, lingered in memory the most, had been what they in the business called 'crimes of passion.' Murder committed out of jealousy or hate or envy or greed or lust; all those sinful things she'd been warned about as a child.

This was the first true crime *without* passion she had ever encountered.

She said as much to Salt as he handed her a glass, refusing one for himself. He was only there to make sure she was okay, not to impose himself. He knew the booze would take the edge off a little, help Angel to sleep. Besides, he was anxious to get home to his own daughters and hold them tight.

"Well," he said, heavily, rubbing his chin and staring at the floor. "I guess there are a whole lot of people in this world, and at some point, we had to meet one like Sylvia."

"She can't be human. Not to do something like that."

"Human or not, she's going to jail for a hell of a long time, Angel. Take comfort in that."

He didn't stay long, just long enough to see Angel finish one glass and move slowly onto the next. He put a hand on her shoulder as he passed her on his way to the door. She patted it with thanks, thinking about a tiny, cold, frail hand of the child they'd found, a child too weak to grip anything.

Leila.

Angel eventually roused herself about an hour after Salt's departure and went over to the stove to reheat some of yesterday's dinner. She moved around her kitchen robotically, doing things but not really seeing, her head full of the stench of Leila's room, a stench she could not seem to stop smelling, even though it had been hours since she had left that damned, evil house.

She laid a place for herself at her small table, and then paused, thinking.

No, not thinking. *Listening* for something.

Then, as if in response to a question, she laid a second placemat at the table. From a cupboard, she retrieved a plastic bowl, a plastic spoon, and a rubber sippy cup. She filled the cup with milk and placed it next to the bowl and spoon.

After that, she went to her bedroom.

On her bed, lay four plump pillows, dressed in freshly laundered, cream-colored pillowcases. She took one from the bed, hugging it to her. Then, she went to her dressing table, took an eyeliner pencil from a bag full of cosmetics, and drew a face onto the pillow. The face was sweet, like a doll's face, with wide eyes rimmed with spidery lashes, and a plump little mouth, and dimples in the cheeks. Angel used lipstick to give the cheeks a faint blush, and eyeshadow to color the eyes a bright blue.

She examined the pillow, frowning a little. It needed something else.

She carried the pillow to her spare room, pushing open the door for the first time in a long time, crossing to a small chest of drawers she kept in there. Opening the top drawer, she pulled out a white cotton dress, small, delicate, unworn—about the right size for a toddler. It had an embroidered hem: a wreath of honeysuckle, hand-stitched. She had sewn that hem herself, pricked her fingers until they bled, every tiny puncture a worthwhile payment for what came at the end.

Or at least, what was *supposed* to come at the end.

Angel pulled the dress on over the pillow, buttoning it up at the neck so that the material and stuffing made a natural head-shaped lump at the top. She held it out at arm's length to examine her handiwork. The Pillow-Baby smiled back at her, and Angel felt something give, inside, a tension that had been building over a long time. It snapped, and there was release. The memories of the starving little girl she'd failed to rescue earlier diminished, just a little. She glanced around the room, a room she hadn't been into for many, many months, a room decorated with a galaxy of wall stickers chosen carefully, after much deliberation, to look as celestial as possible. She took in the stars and clouds and planets and a waning moon, even a tiny rocket, shooting off towards an unknown destination. On the floor, a thick-piled rug lay waiting, and on top of that, in pride of place in the center of the room, stood a cot, with a mobile hanging over the top, more stars dangling down from it. Angel went to the mobile and switched it on. Beethoven's *Fur Elise* tinkled out of the spinning device gently.

"Hi baby," she whispered to the pillow, then. "Hi Leila. Do you like your room?"

The Pillow-Baby stared back at her, unblinking.

Angel carried the pillow to the kitchen, seating it at the table beside her. She spooned out two helpings of dinner, one onto her plate, and one into the plastic bowl before the Pillow-Baby. Then she started to eat, feeling hungry for the first time in weeks. It was good to have an appetite again. It was good to have company while she ate.

And on a windowsill beyond the unlikely pair, a

guttering flame danced on its wick, dipping and bobbing in time to tinkly, mechanical music.

***

After dinner, Angel laid the Pillow-Baby down to sleep in the nursery. Then, she climbed into her own bed. She was one pillow down, but one child up, and that knowledge sent her to sleep more swiftly than she could have imagined possible, given everything she had been through that day.

Before she succumbed to the dark, she rolled onto her back and let her hand slip over her belly, to the soft, pale stripes that runnelled her flesh. She fingered them and thought: *Maybe it wasn't all for nothing, after all.*

***

Angel heard a noise in the night and woke with a start from dreams of terrible things. She lay there for a moment, disoriented, listening. The sound happened again: a murmur, or maybe something else, she couldn't quite make it out.

Either way, it was coming from the direction of Leila's room.

In a daze, Angel shuffled out of her own room and into the nursery, switching on the light, expecting to see the shape of the Pillow-Baby lying on its back in the cot.

Instead, she saw a child, a real, living child, a toddler really, all roly-poly and clean and soft, sitting bolt upright on the mattress, reaching up for the dangling stars that circled in time to Beethoven.

Angel gasped, and the child stopped trying to grab the mobile, looking instead to the woman who stood, frozen in the doorway.

"Leila?"

The two stared at each other for a moment, while Angel tried to understand what was going on. The baby lifted her arms to Angel, her face wreathed in smiles, and held out two chubby arms, happy, pink hands wriggling with her eagerness to be held.

Angel let out a cry of wonder and despair, and crossed the carpet as if in a dream, reaching down, scooping the girl up into her arms, burying her face into Leila's curls, drinking deep of that unique scent that only babies have, well-cared for babies at any rate, a smell of sweetness and delicacy and milk and warmth. The baby chuckled, and Angel held on tighter, her body awash with love and longing. She didn't know what was happening or how, but she knew this was her destiny, somehow. She had been born for this moment; this moment denied to her for so long.

And in a tall mirror hung on the nursery wall, the two figures swayed. Angel's reflection turned. The face of the child she cradled peeked over her shoulder, staring straight into the mirror's shine, only it was not the face of a small, eleven-month-old baby called Leila with blue eyes and soft curls and dimpled cheeks. The thing clutched tight in Angel's arms was not even human. It was ancient and wizened and leathery and wrinkled and hairless. Its hands dangled by its sides, crabbed, old, talons curved wickedly inwards upon balled fists. Its eyes were a piercing bright blue. It was about the same size as a toddler, and clothed in a white cotton dress, with a garland of honeysuckle embroidered around the hem.

Angel didn't seem to notice that the baby's feet ended in claws so sharp they occasionally caught against her bare legs, slashing open her skin, letting loose her blood, which slid down her thighs and calves and found her ankles just like it had that day, that damned day when her round, parturient belly had suddenly tightened, and then tightened again, as if an electric current were running through her body, the current of life, and at first she didn't think much of it, she had been told to expect this in the weeks leading up to her date, but the pain of her contractions had hit her, then, like a train at full speed: *wham, wham, wham, wham*, forcing her to her knees, fast, it was too fast, it wasn't supposed to happen like this! It was supposed to take time, she was supposed to have *time*, everyone said that it could take days, sometimes, to give birth, not like this, not like this, oh god, she hadn't even packed a hospital bag, and she knew she should wait for an ambulance or for help before she pushed, but she was alone, Angel was *always* alone, and the baby wouldn't wait, it *couldn't* wait, her body was no longer able to...to…

"Oh god," Angel said, rocking the strange creature in her arms. "Oh, god." And in her mind, she recalled the sensation of being forced apart, pulled asunder like soft, ripped cheese, and there was pain, and blood, and more blood, so much blood, and other things she didn't understand, an umbilical cord, maybe, but it was hard to tell, her vision was clouded with pain, and her baby, oh, her sweet, sweet baby…

Never opened her eyes.

Angel began to cry, pressing her cheek to the cheek of

the creature. Her tears dripped onto its leathery skin. A wide, wizened mouth opened in the thing's face, revealing a dark slit. Out of this, a long, thin tongue slowly emerged, exploring the region around its mean lips, finding the salty wetness of Angel's grief, and lapping it up like a thirsty cat drinking cream.

And they danced, then, on the nursery floor, the nursery that should have belonged to Angel's baby, a baby she had named Leila in the last few tremulous moments of the little girl's existence, and the name was beautiful, just like Leila had been, sweet baby Leila, who never had a chance, who now lived amongst the stars.

The thing that was *not* Angel's dead daughter—or the coincidentally named child from the filthy house full of barbecue smoke and death that Angel had been dispatched to the day before—shuddered in pleasure, enjoying the sensation of being held, enjoying the warmth of a mother denied her bond. It made a low crooning noise deep in its throat, and dug its claws deeper into the soft flesh of Angel's legs.

Her skin turned a dark, rusty red.

Soon, they were dancing on a floor flooded with grief.

TROUBLE WITH FATE

Sarah Read

Ill-wishing always leaves me fuzzy-brained. Like I'm trying to think through pudding. I like to think I'd've seen trouble coming, elsewise—but there are no portents to be seen in the glow of a washcloth draped over one's own face.

I've been told the headache is my punishment—a part of it. Small part, really. That there's more to come. But that's from folks who may not understand just what heaps of adrenaline and intense focus can do. I may have earned this pain, but not for moral reasons. I'd argue that's arbitrary.

But just the same, punishment or not, Trouble found me.

Trouble had a voice like gravel slung in a silk hanky.

"Maybelle wants to see you." He smiled his troublesome smile.

"Of course she does. How long did it take you to find me this time?"

"Eight years."

It had been a good eight years. No Trouble. Far from my sisters.

"You're getting better." I pulled the cloth from my face and sat up, the pain in my head beating fresh as I shifted.

"You're getting sloppy."

It was the ill-wish. I was sure. You don't send

58

something like that out into the universe without leaving a trail. I'd sent up a cosmic flair for Trouble to follow.

"Yeah, sure. Where are we going this time?" She's always sending Trouble for me. And Trouble always finds me, sooner or later.

"Edinburgh."

"Ugh. And when?"

"1512."

"Jesus."

He held out his hand for me. His nails looked like wasp wings left on the windowsill too long.

I grabbed my bag—mostly for the hand sanitizer (Trouble's hands are in everything), and took his hand. We took two steps back, and I turned around to see Maybelle standing in front of a polished silver dish, a servant behind her brushing her black hair all the way to her heels. She was naked except for a rope of beads that crisscrossed her body, tangling in her flowing hair. Her skin was tiger striped with soft scarring, her stomach draped in loose crepe ripples across her front.

"Adrenaline. Sister, it's good to see you," she said.

My name sounds prettier the way we say it. But it's appropriate enough, the way it's used nowadays.

"Why must we always meet where there are no engines?" The room smelled of hot lard candles and wood smoke. Slow burns.

"Because you'd drive off." She waved her hand and the servant backed out of the room. Trouble settled himself in a corner. He's never far from Maybelle. "Adrenaline, come back to us. We have work to do—Father's work—and we need our third to get it done."

"I'm not interested in Father's work."

"That doesn't matter. He left it to us." The beads chimed as she spun to me. Her eyes were as black as her hair, no sclera—just pits of night in her face. She could drive a mortal off a cliff with a look. Had done. She could make a fortune in my line of work, but she preferred prophecy. Or, writing books that few would read and fewer understand, and fewer still believe. She insisted that it was not a waste of time—that humans would see, in the end.

Yeah, the end. As in, too late. She might not even have time for an "I told you so."

"It's your unfinished work, now."

"So? I have unfinished work back home, too. Unfinished work everywhere. I like to stay busy."

Trouble nodded his agreement from the corner.

"You don't want to die with unfinished work on your conscience."

Somehow I knew she was looking deep into me. As if the blackness of her eyes were making itself at home in my heart.

"Die?" It was the strangest thing she'd ever said. "We don't die."

She turned to Trouble. "Perhaps you'd like to explain this one."

He leapt from the corner stool, ever eager, and sauntered over, began gathering Maybelle's hair into a plait. Most would have lost their arms for touching her, but Trouble always could get away with more.

"You can. You might. All of you. She's seen it."

Mention of her gift usually brought a smile to Maybelle's lips, but instead they seemed paler.

"And what should be the cause of our downfall? What

power is there to snuff the three weird sisters? Who besides Father ever commanded such destruction?"

She held out her bare ivory hands, fingers overlong and beckoning for mine.

I rubbed the engine grease from my palms onto my jeans and took her hands.

"Sister. Daughter. You do."

***

AllysaAndrina's tongue had grown so dry in her papery mouth that we had to push the bone paste down her throat with our own fingers.

"We need you, sister," Maybelle said. She cleaned her fingers with her hair.

I reached into the crisp pit of Ally's nose and grasped a silver hair, jerked it free.

The ropes that suspended her over her pedestal snapped and her narrow, knotted fingers circled my throat.

"Oh good, you're awake," I choked through her bone grip.

"I was busy." She breathed dust across my face and I felt it settle on my eyes, against my teeth.

Maybelle's pale fingers caressed her grip and the dark stars dispersed from my vision.

"Allysa, there has been a prophecy."

"I know."

"About Adrenaline."

"About us all."

"You've seen it?" Maybelle's brow drew down. She did not like to share her gift.

Allysa turned her empty eyes toward Maybelle and grasped her hair. She brought the plaited tresses to her mouth and licked the bone paste residue, her tongue like a long-dead mouse.

"I wrote it," she said. "Of course, then, it was about me. But now I am this." She turned to me again. I flinched as she raised her hands, but this time it was my breasts she grabbed. "I remember these, oh yes. Now these are yours, and so is the prophecy."

"What do we do? We must stop it?" Maybelle's face had flushed and it occurred to me—for the first time in millennia—that she did in fact care for me. That I was hers, once. That she probably still thought so. And I felt, for a moment, the first stirring of worry for myself—her worry. And I felt safer, knowing this harridan fought on my side.

"You don't need me, sisters, daughters. Not yet. Not anymore. I'll be there at my time. At the end." As she spoke, she slid effortlessly back onto her pedestal. She dragged strands of Maybelle's hair with her and used them to affix herself in place.

"Surely we can change this course. We are fate! We decide all paths." Maybelle grasped at AllysaAndrina's rags.

"And we did. I did. This is the path I set long ago. Now follow it, sister-daughters, and I will meet you at the end."

Some absent light left her eyes and she returned to her rest—or to her work—whichever task diverted her ancient mind.

***

Maybelle paced, Trouble at her heels, matching her step-for-step over the uneven stones of the floor.

"I need to see more. I need more detail about what's coming so we can try to stop it."

"It doesn't sound like we can stop it." I was experiencing the unique relief of powerlessness—of letting go and floating with the current, whether it carried me to a calm lagoon or over the edge. I suppose there's always an edge, eventually, beyond the lagoon.

"Trouble, bring me a mirror, some ice—a pound of it—and some hemlock tea."

Trouble's smile unnerved me. "I'll make your tea," I said. "I don't think you want Trouble brewing your toxic tea."

I suppose, of all the advances in building and architecture, the kitchen is the least changed over time. And the kettle unchanged at all. I brewed the tea to a concentration just shy of deadly and scowled at a cup of water till it froze. Slower than a man's heart.

Maybelle assembled her kit and began sipping her tea. "Now leave me. I need quiet for this."

I left the old stone house and set off on a path across the field. The sky of the past always felt more open than my own sky—as if the airplanes and satellites weighed down my shoulders, somehow. As if the sky here were aware of its wilderness.

I picked my way over broad rocks speckled with small yellow flowers and around bristled shrubs. Trouble followed.

***

A cluster of thorn trees had colonized a hollow in the stony landscape. They grew up and over an ancient stone circle that had fallen out of alignment. Its broken barrier rang like a bell in my ears, but I climbed atop one anyway and sat, staring into the shadows beneath the wind-stunted trees.

Trouble was still somewhere close, but our paths had diverged. Doubtless he was off laming a horse or setting a rockslide.

The trees at the center of the broken circle stirred and two hands emerged. "I'm sorry," a voice followed. A tattered head followed the voice. The nest of hair was as brambled as the thorn trees and the lichen-colored eyes were barely visible through the mess.

"You're sorry?"

The man still held his hands aloft. "I didn't want to scare you," he said.

"I'm not scared of you."

"Oh." He lowered his hands and began climbing out of the thorns. They plucked at the dark kilt that was all he wore. "Good." He scaled the rock that was next to mine.

He was younger than he had first appeared. What I had taken for age lines were simply streaks of mud.

"You picked a strange place to rest, thorn-hollow-man."

He nodded, his wild hair and beard accentuating the movement. "And yet, you rest here, too."

"And the noise doesn't bother you?"

"Noise?"

He couldn't hear the scream of the broken circle. Just a mortal, then. A simple madman.

"The wind, howling like it does?"

"Oh, that—no. Good as music, to me."

Definitely mad. But well-formed, I noted, his wanderings having carved him into a roughness that appealed to the ancient in me. "Have you been here long?"

He pulled at his beard, smoothing the hairs down into something more civilized. "I suppose I have." He looked down at the nest of hair in his hand. "Don't remember having this."

Not just a madman, but a cursed one. A young, chiseled Lear.

I reached into my jacket pocket and handed him a plastic comb.

"What's this, then?"

Ah. I had forgotten we'd left my time. It's impossible to tell on the moor, where change is measured geologically.

"Here. Let me help." I leaned across the space between our stones and began pulling the comb through his wild hair, removing thorns and leaves and even small rocks. Patches of lichen that had rooted to his scalp. He smelled like the stones and the small purple flowers that blanket them in spring.

"That's kind of you, miss."

It was more selfish of me. He was well enough without, but I wanted to see more of him. Find out how he came to be spell-trapped in a broken stone circle.

I pulled him down from the stone and rubbed the dirt from his skin with a fistful of dry grass, cleaned the clay from his nails with tree thorns. I cleared the sleep from his eyes with caresses. I cleared the spell from his mind with a wild romp in the bracken that shook the grouse and plover from their nests for miles.

I left him sleeping there in the circle, the spell once again taking hold, wilderness growing over him like a warm blanket.

Trouble joined me outside the circle, and I realized he'd been there all along. His grin was overwide and his teeth overlong and twisted like the broken stone circle.

We walked in silence and returned to find Maybelle asleep on the cold stone floor in front of her mirror. Trouble woke her.

"Adrenaline? Daughter, where are you?"

"Here," I said, and touched her wrist. I had never seen her so tired. Never seen the lines in her face hold onto their shadows the way they did now.

She lifted herself on her soft arms. "We need to get you out of this time and away from here."

"Damn straight."

"No—this is where it happens. The act that unmakes us." Her hands climbed me, making their way to my face. She pressed them to my cheeks. Even her stone-chilled palms felt warm against my wind-kissed skin. "Where have you been? What have you done?" Her voice was crumbling, the lines around her pit-eyes arching and twisting.

"It is done," Trouble said.

Maybelle looked as if she might scream, but instead she folded, her hands slipping from my face. "It is done," she repeated.

"Done? What is?" My confusion was creeping into alarm. "If we need to go, let's go!"

"There's no point in going, now. It is as

AllysaAndrina said. The path is set. We must walk it. And meet our sister-mother at the end."

***

I stared into Maybelle's mirror, searching for my own face in the mess of shadows flitting by. "I didn't know that could even happen." I ran my fingers over the front of my shirt, as if there were any chance I might already feel the quickening there.

"The Maiden never does. Never thinks it will." Maybelle lay back against a velvet pillow and closed her eyes, her face now crossed with lines like the thorn bracken on the moor.

"Do you remember your first?"

"We were all my first. I was always this…I think. I don't remember a time when my arms were empty or my breasts dry."

"We must have begun somehow."

"Allysa seems to know something of it. At least in riddles."

"She's not being super helpful."

"She exists to be served now, not to serve."

"She barely exists at all."

"Soon, none of us will."

The sudden sour heat in my throat might have been fear, or regret, or the thing inside me. "I'm sorry…"

"It's not your fault. You couldn't have known. We couldn't have predicted this."

"Allysa could, apparently."

"Yes. Well. As you said…not 'super helpful.'" She cast aside her ropes of beads and pulled a soft robe over her sagging belly.

"Does it hurt?"

"What, dying? How should I know?"

"No, this thing." I turned sideways. Was my stomach bigger? Would it sag like Maybelle's?

"Yes. It does."

I wanted to scream and curse and rage, but for the first time in my long stretch of existence, I felt impotent. Like I could raise the sea or turn the sun to stone and it would mean nothing. A pointless fraction of what I felt. I wanted to ride. I needed speed—to outrun this path laid at my feet or ride it over the edge at my own pace.

"I still want to go back to my time. My place. I want to die at home."

"I don't think that's a good idea," Maybelle said.

"Why the fuck not?" I might raise fire, instead. Vent the raging mantle of the earth.

"Because this has happened here and now. In your time—it may already be over. Your time might not even be there, now."

***

A hammer isn't a wrench, but it was all I had. The wrench wouldn't be invented for two hundred years. Or maybe not at all.

The banded wagon wheels weren't perfectly round, nor the roads smooth. I had nothing to construct gears or brakes, but I could push with my feet, and—just for a moment—feel speed on my face.

"Should you be doing that?" Trouble asked. Just as he spoke, the wheel hit a rut and I toppled to the side into a patch of gorse.

"Why should it matter? Doesn't seem to matter what I do or don't decide."

Trouble smiled and helped me to my feet. "If the baby comes ahead of time, so does the end."

Something about his words struck me. Something about new life and the end of things. I walked my bicycle home, Trouble ten steps behind me.

***

I had felt pain before. I was no stranger to it. But this was enormous. This pain felt universal, sentient. As though I had been unmade and remade.

My back arched and ground against the slick stone floor. The flood from between my legs rushed between the stones, soaking my hair. My screams echoed through the dark passages.

AllysaAndrina stared down at me from the pedestal, choking and chanting. Maybelle knelt at my head, holding my hands, sobbing. Trouble crouched between my knees, grinning as he pulled something wet and dark from my center.

He placed the creature in my arms. Her skin and eyes were blue, but then her tiny lips parted—her complexion brightened as a wail to rival my own split the air.

"Here is your tiny maiden, mother. And here is the daughter of your daughter."

AllysaAndrina's chanting stopped and the stones in the walls fractured, raining sand and dust that stuck to the slick, wet skin of the mewling baby.

My breasts began to tingle and burn. Golden milk

flowed in rivulets. The tiny maiden's screams grew more insistent, and I scooped her up and held her to my flowing breast. She took the nipple in her mouth and began to drink. Trouble took the other side.

AllysaAndrina's figure—stone, now, on the plinth—gazed down on us. The mother, maiden, and crone, remade for a new age, and nursing Trouble.

A KEY FOR ANY LOCK

S.H. Cooper

I was a smart girl. Everyone said so.

From the time I was a child, testing out different methods to build up static electricity for science fairs, to when I was accepted into university to study mechanical engineering. It was always one of the first things people said about me.

Such a smart, smart girl.

But I never heard it more than after That Night.

"You're a smart girl; why did you dress that way?"

"You're a smart girl; why did you drink so much?"

"You're a smart girl; why were you alone with him?"

Nobody asked him why he'd kept insisting on giving me drinks. No one asked him why he followed me into the upstairs bedroom when I excused myself to lie down. No one asked him why, for such a smart boy, he was so fucked up.

It was *me* who should've known better. Done better. He had a reputation, you see. Not one you should judge him by, mind you, especially not if you were one of those fine folks on the jury. Didn't he look so respectable in his fitted suit, standing there with his gaggle of attorneys, head bowed, sorry I regretted my "decision," but innocent, Your Honor.

I'd made the report. I'd had the examinations. I'd let them poke and prod my tender parts with their tools and their eyes and their questions. I'd been sexually active, they'd said. But that didn't prove anything beyond a reasonable doubt. College girls at college parties will do what college girls do, and it wasn't like this was the first time I'd had myself a little fun. They had some old flings to testify to that fact.

My side had our own evidence, including a slew of telling social media posts. They flashed up on a projector, his smiling picture beside his philosophizing: *somebody asked why only women can be sluts. Its cuz a lock that opens for any key is useless but a key that opens any lock? Priceless.*

He was very fond of that analogy. Women as locks, him as a skeleton key, destined to open them all. He repeated this same sentiment in a number of different ways with a number of different words, always to a seemingly endless stream of Likes. He even added "The Key" as his middle name on his profile.

But it was just a tasteless joke, he said.

In the end, it was my word against his.

His just came out of more expensive mouthpieces.

We did the whole song and dance, but it felt like he'd been given the steps ahead of time, and he outpaced me. At least, that's what the verdict said.

"We, the jury, find the defendant to be 'not guilty.'"

It didn't take long for the anonymous phone calls, texts, and private messages to start. They called me names, said I was trying to ruin a good guy's life, told me to kill myself. The faceless masses dubbed my case "The Lock and Key Trial" and crude pictures of an anthropomorphic padlock dripping white from her keyhole were spread around online. Every inbox I had flooded with abuse until it felt like there was no way to escape it.

Campus no longer felt safe.

The friends I thought I'd had frittered away.

My world became very small, utterly tainted by That Night.

Time heals all wounds, it's said, but I find that's more true if you weren't the one cut in the first place. While everyone else moved on, distanced themselves from the damaged goods, I was left to nurse my hurt alone.

Nobody likes a liar, and with just two words, the court had made me a plagued jester.

Mom and Dad suggested I move home for a while, let things settle down, maybe even take the rest of the year off, but that felt like admitting defeat. *I* wasn't the one who should be made to leave!

Truth be told, though, I couldn't stay either.

So I started driving. Long, aimless road trips where I could exist outside of being The Lock.

That's when I found the old farmhouse.

I'd turned off the highway, followed the winding country lanes, and left behind any semblance of life. The farmhouse was barely visible from the road, down an overgrown path I'd discovered when I was trying to find a place to turn around again. It was clear from the rot and collapsing roof that it hadn't been used in some time.

I parked in front of it, studying its sagging frame through my windshield before I pushed open my door and stepped out. Even from a distance, there was a damp, musty odor to the place. The stillness that surrounded it, interrupted only by the drone of unseen cicadas, was unlike anything I'd experienced before. The sense of utter aloneness, of being forgotten, seemed steeped into the very soil. I circled it slowly, studying its tired windows and decaying walls, running my fingers lightly along the uneven wood. Perhaps it had been red once, like in all the picture books, but age and neglect had turned it a splintered brown.

I stopped short when I rounded the back, a surprised gasp escaping me.

They were scattered across the ground, partially reclaimed by the tall grass. Green blades grew over bleached white, pierced empty sockets, forced their way through slack jaws.

Skulls. Cow, maybe. Some kind of farm animal, anyway, left, as the house had been. A graveyard of unfortunate creatures with no one to tend it. I doubted anyone even knew they were there. Or cared. Why would they? They were just animals after all, probably slaughtered for some "greater purpose." And it wasn't like anyone was checking up on the house to know of their existence.

All the way out here.

So isolated.

That's when I started coming up with my plan.

I didn't put it into motion right away. I had to be patient, gather my supplies. Cash-only purchases spread out over the next year across different towns I visited: an expensive wig from one, realistic temporary tattoos from a couple others, knee-high boots that were a size up, skimpy clothes that were a size down, colored contacts. And all the bits and bobs I'd need to build it.

It shouldn't have been as easy as it was. Especially not since I was using his own tactics. I sidled up alongside him at a house party, my smile cool and coy while my heart jackhammered against my ribs. I expected him to recognize me at any moment, to see past all the contour and brunette bangs, recognize the hatred burning behind the dark lenses covering my natural blue. But all he saw was the ample cleavage spilling over my tube top, the butterfly tramp stamp when I danced against him.

I'm not sure he realized I even had a face.

His nearness, the stench of his breath, the grating sound of his laughter. Every touch came as a wasp sting. I imagined my skin reddening beneath his fingers, breaking out in hives, rising in hideous bumps, and all I wanted to do was claw at my own flesh until there was nothing left of him on me.

Endure, I told myself after dodging yet another sloppy kiss under the guise of playfulness. *Endure.*

The drinks kept coming; I made sure of it. He downed them all without ever wondering why I never had to refill my own cup.

We stumbled out together just after midnight, a seemingly drunken pair on their way to more debauchery. I didn't have a car, I told him. I'd come with friends. No problem, he replied. He had his. I snatched the keys from his fumbling fingers, plucked his cell phone from his pocket, and pushed him into the backseat. He tried to protest, only he got to drive his baby, but the words came out in a slurred string as he tipped and swayed. I dropped his phone on the ground and slid into the driver's seat.

He was asleep before we made it halfway to the farmhouse.

Getting him inside was a challenge. He was dead weight and I had to haul him inch by inch through the dark and the dirt. He stank of cheap beer and piss. I grit my teeth and let my fury transform me into a lioness, a black widow, a she-wolf baring her fangs and dragging her still-kicking prey towards her lair.

We made it into the farmhouse, pitch-black until I found the lamp I'd left by the door. Its light was intentionally dim, offering little more than shapes and outlines to see by, but maintaining anonymity. No undue attention needed.

I slapped him until he stirred enough to help me stand him upright.

He grinned like an idiot while I stripped him, giggled when I pushed his arms up over his head and closed the manacles around his wrists, never registering the cold metal pressing against his naked front. His bout of consciousness didn't last, and he slumped, held upright by the chains, while I took a seat on the ground in front of him.

When he finally opened his eyes and the confusion became murky understanding that something wasn't right, but he wasn't yet sure just how wrong it was, I allowed myself to smile. He looked down at me and demanded to know who I was, what was going on, where he was. The usual questions, I suppose.

I came to stand in front of him, separated by the contraption between us. I rested both hands upon its smooth surface and stroked it affectionately. He followed my gaze down to it.

A giant padlock, its keyhole level with his groin.

He sputtered, demanding to know what was going on and that I unlock the restraints, and this time I obliged with an answer.

"I'm not going to hurt you," I said. "Actually, I'm just

going to leave you here."

There was some name calling, some chain rattling, attempts at intimidation. But I was over being scared, especially of him.

"You can get out on your own," I assured him when he took a breath. "You just have to want it."

The look he gave me was a dumb one.

"You have the key to any lock on you at all times. You say so yourself. This one is no different."

Finally, finally, horrified comprehension began to creep into his face, pulling his eyes wide and his mouth into an "o". He looked down at the padlock pressing so close to his midsection again.

It was a simple design, a plain metal face with a circular opening pointed toward him. Solid, strong, but innocuous enough save for its size, far larger than the typical ones I'd based it on. The kind of nondescript lock you might find in any hardware store, save all the wire and tubes running from it to his shackles.

And what was in it, of course. All those gears and turning parts.

All those hungry, sharp edges.

"All you have to do is use your key," I said, fingers caressing the lock. "Granted, it'll be the last time you do. Some locks are just so...temperamental. Unforgiving. But it'll be worth it, won't it? You'll be free."

The implications were setting in and he yanked his hips back, twisting to the side with one leg raised defensively.

"What's the matter? It'll just be a moment of pain. A bit of blood. A lifetime of memories." Bitterness seeped into words, tore at their corners, turning them into jagged little knives flung from my throat. "But you'll be alive. You can move on, live up to all that potential I hear you have."

I stepped back, taking a deep breath to steady myself. "At least I'm giving you the chance to make a choice."

He yanked at his manacles, screaming I was a bitch, a psycho, while I walked toward the door. I wondered, after all was said and done, would I care? If the cops showed up on my door because he'd made the choice and managed to drag himself away from this ruin. Or if his withered ghost, cursed with hunger and thirst and hate, followed me to the end of my days.

Would I care?

Why was I doing this to him?

His question made me stop walking. Stop wondering. I half-turned, lips pulled back into a gallows smile.

"Because I'm a smart girl, and I knew no one else would."

THE CURSE OF SHE, PART 6:
THE FINAL GIRLFRIEND

Hailey Piper

You have a role to play, so play it.

These are the glitz and glamor days, the silver screen full of stars, both shooting and falling. You're no star; you're an archetype, a void they travel through—don't fret about the actresses though. They're not why you're here. Play your role, and you'll never be forgotten.

The theater fills, your audience chewing, yowling, demanding, their behavior in mimicry of a horror sub-genre yet unborn. Beastly as they are, you do it for them. So, do it.

It's a monster movie—isn't it always?—and there's a creature on the loose. You'll meet him before a monochrome card flashes across the screen and reads, The End. For now, play the lover, either a girlfriend full of smiles or an unsure paramour to be won over by the hero's charm at a dramatic moment.

Never a wife, understand? Joe Hollywood has checked the screening surveys, and the charts never lie: wife characters don't resonate with audiences. Low appeal.

You're a lover, so fall in love with the hero. The more characters in the movie like him, the more the audience will like him too, so says almighty Aristotle. Repeat the holy mantra: you have a role to play, so play it.

But what's love without its rival? He's coming,

remember? Time to meet the monster.

He never looks the same. Sometimes he wears a cloak and brandishes fangs, or he's covered in scales, or he has bolts coming out of his neck, or he's a mad scientist in a lab coat that shines in black and white. Either way, he's going to carry you off in the climax, and you'll have two jobs here:

1. Give your hero something heroic to do by rescuing you.

2. Give him his reward for reaching the movie's finale alive. Remember, the climax belongs to him. It's not yours. You just work here.

The End.

For a time, it's enough to grace the silver screen at all. Other genres exist, other roles, but they're not for you, and who would want them? The western has a short shelf life. War flicks barely think on you. But horror, monster movies, those thriller chillers that draw up the skeletons from every audience's closet? They'll endure. And they'll always need a girlfriend, a lover. A victim.

But after countless monsters, rescues, and heroic final kisses, the disparity of what's his and what's yours gets old. You want to do something heroic in the climax. You might even like to be the hero yourself.

Joe Hollywood hears you out, but he's no boat-rocker, else audiences might begin to flop into the sea and find other things to do. He'll bribe you with gifts. Here, let's replace that drab monochrome with a little technicolor. Have a few wardrobe shifts to suit the times. Every gal likes to be a little sexier, yeah? Some attitude can't hurt; it'll only make the hero more appealing when he wins you over from your shrewish ways, your personality dribbling away with the vanquished monster's blood at the climax.

Yes, it plays out the same. At the end of the day, you're the girlfriend, the lover. The monster will carry you off, and the hero will save you. Risk, reward, resolution. The End.

Until the story turns.

Joe Hollywood didn't warn you in advance, and why would he? Knowing the plan was never your role. Sometimes you can't be sure there's a plan at all.

The narrative shift is subtle at first, a slight turning of the screw in the same old structure. In the beginning, the monsters change. Say goodbye to rubber suits and mad scientists, hello to creepy masks and brutal murder. Chocolate syrup for blood went the way of the dinosaur when Joe Hollywood crumpled up monochrome and tossed it into last week. This stuff's redder than the real thing.

You don't realize just how red until one of those masked men jams a knife in your gut. That reddest red spills out of you. Your hero is due any moment though, right? That's his job in the climax. You'll be rescued, and you'll reward him all the better for saving you from this red.

Only, he doesn't show up. This isn't even the climax yet; you're the bottom of the second act, wishing you'd crawled a few celluloid frames further. He can't rescue you now. Your job was to let him, and you've failed. How can he rescue a dead woman?

He doesn't. Instead, he avenges you. His new job is to kill the monster.

The End.

That must have been a fluke, you think. Joe

Hollywood decided to rock the boat a little after all. Surely audiences can't accept this.

But they do. They eat it up, and they're back for seconds. The culture's changing out there, and the silver screen will be its mirror. You're not a reward anymore. Your new job is to die. Purity reigns, and to be the lover is to be impure. The Book of Genesis flexes its muscles, or at least Joe Hollywood's interpretation.

You had a role to play, and you played it, and you wanted more, and now you get less. Shouldn't you be grateful you have a role at all? Maybe your has-been eyes didn't notice, but there's a new girl in town. Someone else, a friend to the girlfriend, but she's no lover. This one's pure and untainted, a Virgin Mary to your Eve, and while you bleed to death in a thousand horrific ways, she sees the end credits. The girlfriend is old news; you've been replaced.

They call her the final girl.

She doesn't play the hero, not really, but she outlasts him, and more importantly, she outlasts the monster. She outlasts you. Dead and done two scenes before the climax, you watch helpless from the celluloid grave as the final girl is hunted and brutalized and stained red with fake blood, but despite her suffering, she survives the climax.

Sometimes, she even wins.

Who the hell does she think she is? This was never your story, but at least you had a role to play, and you played it. Time and again, from silence to sound to color, you earned survival to the end title card or the end credits, depending on the cinematic era. You had so little to begin with, but she's taken even that.

"Come on, baby, you still got roles," Joe Hollywood

says. "Sometimes you'll live. We'll even throw in a rescue now and then for old time's sake."

He puts on a winning smile, but he's looking impatient these days. He doesn't want to keep having these chats with you when he has bigger and better trinkets to lure in audiences. Back in the day, you would see the monster, faint off your feet, and be carried away. Now you endure the brutality of new filmmakers, unrestrained from past manners and decency.

And back in the day, you never looked across film reels and spotted her. That final girl.

Why should she get what you never got? You put in your dues facing off against every Frankenstein, Dracula, and King Kong that reared his ugly public domain head. Original, remake, or something between, you played your role.

And yet the final girl reaps the rewards. She's the fresh starlight in Joe Hollywood's eye.

If only one of you can take the spotlight, it's not going to be her. Hot jealousy burns inside you, searing holes through film reels. In theaters across the world, the people manning the projection booths have to apologize to frustrated audiences. "Something's wrong with the light," or "We lost a couple frames." Theater managers offer free tickets in recompense, and the picture resumes. The show must go on.

Each time they push the film forward, sacrificing those seconds you've burned away, you lose a little screen time. You're there a little less.

The sacrifice will be worth it, you promise yourself. When the gap in film hangs wide enough, you'll reach across the silver screen, to movies you were never part of, where you were never needed, and you'll grab that final girl by the throat. Switch your places. She can put in dues as the girlfriend for a few decades, and you can outlast the monster, play the hero, and see the end credits again. You'll have your climax.

After years of burning celluloid across vast popcorn plains and spilled soda lakes, your fingers snag the frame's edge of a faraway film. There's no girlfriend in this picture, you won't find an easy role to slide inside, but you've crossed over. There will be a role for you once you take the mantle of final girl for yourself.

You stalk her scene by scene. Sometimes you're watching just off-screen, and other times you're two steps behind her. She's panicked, almost like the monster is on her heels, but you'll reach her first. The movie counts down its remaining frames. Here comes the climax.

But when you arrive, it's just you and her. No monster. What kind of horror movie is this?

And then you realize. You're the alien from another world, the beast from below. You've crossed frames and films to reach her, and who else chases the final girl with that level of narrative absolute?

Forget Eve. To the final girl's Virgin Mary, you're the Devil, spurned and hated and vengeful. A demon.

The monster.

But that doesn't mean you win now. You're together at last, and yet the final girl cuts you down in the end. The climax belongs to both of you, but the end result still isn't fair. Joe Hollywood has pitted you against each other, and no matter which film reel, she wins. Audience, climax, end credits—she gets it all. Why did you expect any different if you shared this part of the film? She's the final girl; it's in her title. You're just a girlfriend who doesn't know her place, a monster in the making all along.

Jealousy ignites to a supernova flare. Holes burn across movies once more, though now instead of scorched film cans, you bring data corruption to digital projectors. Audiences adjust to these technical blips. At worst, they knock a star off their online review, and the silver screen is full of stars. Joe Hollywood has sunk his fair share of galaxies.

You can keep reaching across the movies, but what is there to find? There's no place for you anymore. You're a ghost, haunting the void between films, a haunted house's backstory.

Still, there's power in this role. Not much, but maybe the climax can be yours.

The final girl, she's used to fighting monsters, but this is different. She gathers priests, witches, incantations, Ouija boards, childhood songs to no avail. She digs through the movie's every resource for clues, your spectral silver bullet, that key element of backstory that might save the day. Just what is your unfinished business?

Oh, so *now* she wants to know you. *Now* she cares.

There are no blueprints for this plot device, and sometimes the plot abandons all logic entirely. Gone is the technobabble of your heyday; cinematic nonsense isn't all that different, and it gets the job done. Who needs sense? Audiences crave a victim, and you'll give them one.

Frayed narrative threads form a garrote in your hands. You waste no time twisting it around her neck.

You kill the final girl.

The title is empty, a default moniker she keeps by

grace of being the last to die. She's possessed, or drowned, or sucked into unspeakable darkness, never to be seen again by the audience. Down the deep holes you've burned through movies.

The climax is yours. At last.

Jealousy mellows to room temperature in the void between films and film stars. Victory tastes like tap water. Why aren't you satisfied? This is what you wanted. You've slain the final girl, dead in your ghostly arms story after story.

And then her head turns in a way it never has before. Her lips part, and not for the character. She sees you across films, the way you've been seeing her.

The final girl speaks: "What are you doing to my movies?"

What's that feeling inside? Not hot jealousy, but cold like you've never known, a frozen rock that hurts your heart.

Shame.

She isn't a character of many faces. She's an archetype, like you, with a history that's both real and reel. Just because she's younger and less experienced doesn't make her care about her role any less.

You sit with her between films, and for once, you talk together. You tell her where you come from, about the movies you've starred in, your time as the girlfriend since the days of silent film, your dissatisfaction, your desires.

And she tells you what she's been through. She's tired of being brutalized, of killing the monster, of watching loved ones die over and over. Most of all, she's tired of being alone. In the same way that her birth took away what little you had, your invasion has taken what little was hers.

You realize you've lost sight of what you wanted from the start. Not just to see the end credits, but to have mattered for them. You used to ask Joe Hollywood if you could be the hero, and instead he let you die. You thrust that pain at the final girl, but was she the one who really deserved it?

By the end of your long talk, you're both crying and holding each other's hands.

What do you do now? You ponder that while audiences grow restless. They want their archetypes and tropes. Where the hell are you? Who do you think you belong to, if not them? Both of you need to crawl out of your misery hole and get back on the silver screen. Remember, the show must go on. You have roles to play, so play them.

Instead, you both girlfriend-turned-monster and final girl-turned-victim reach deeper into each other's arms, your forms twining into amalgamations of past and present. Were anyone to see through the screens to your truest forms, they might mistake the two of you as merging into one.

But you're not of one form, only of purpose. A contradictory singularity that remains multitudinous, and what is more appropriate to your conflicting roles than a contradiction? Every incarnation lives within you. No Mary, Eve, or Devil—you are Legion, for you are many, a collective coven that twists cinema into a needful black hole.

And the plot twists with it.

The movie isn't sure what to make of you at first. Which part of your new conglomeration is girlfriend, victim, monster, or final girl? You can't answer; you aren't sure yourselves. There is no separation, and yet you are all of these things.

Some of the audience turns restless. Why don't you do what you used to do? They liked that. It was familiar, nostalgic. They're attuned to ways of Joe Hollywood, but you aren't going to let things play out the way they always have.

A new climax awaits you, a field not laced in popcorn and soda, but in blood and death.

You are the final girl not by incident, the monster not by tragedy. Fate turns because your hand-turned-claw grabs hold of power. You are queens and witches and blood-soaked brides. You are She, for you are the many that is one.

The climax is yours at last. Every beat of self-assurance ripples through the audience, a resonance washing across the hearts of everyone who has seen herself, even briefly, thrust into the role of victim, girlfriend, final girl, or monster. Each feels your contradiction, and for once, she is known. And that sense of being known binds her to your She-Legion, a narrative thread that winds around her heart long after the end credits roll.

A unified howl rages down those threads, through those hearts, and in this instant, you too are known. There's a climax after the credits, beyond the film, and though you were unaware of its shape, you've wanted it from the days of chatting with Joe Hollywood for more. You now crave a reward he wouldn't or couldn't give you even before you dragged your thousand claws across his throat. Let the world forget him. Old news buried under a parking lot between the theater and a gas station.

Look instead to the age of new and beautiful monsters, both gracing the silver screen and emerging in the audience. Here rises the reward you've been waiting for all these years. You hadn't noticed it through countless celluloid frames, but now it burns brighter than any climax or end credits.

It is that final shot that draws the curtain, a close-up of your broken and universal face, the moment you come into your power, and every heart in your thrall feels it.

Absolution.

THE MUTATION OF ALMOST BEAUTIFUL THINGS

Sara Tantlinger

You were beautiful once, rare with fluttering wings of
exquisite patterns, a shimmer all your own. You
cherished yourself and understood how to be alone, and
maybe deep down you can find that again, but dear girl,
you're going to have to dig deep.

See the carving knife? Take it.
Cut off your wings
because they are not yours anymore.
You gave them away for the sake of pretty lies,
and you can't handle flying anymore.
Cut off your wings, eat the shimmer,
and see if it can cover up the ugly ways
your ragged heart beats inside raw ribs.

Slice off your little legs, you must relearn to crawl, you
must go back to the cocoon.

Hide yourself, hide away, all the other butterflies are
dead, but you didn't care because you had a companion,
didn't you?

The butterflies are dead
what have you done?

Go back to the cocoon and wait for a bird to swallow
you. Let yourself be reborn inside its stomach, and
maybe you'll find peace between the innards.

This is what you have done.
You must kill all the parts
that you gave away to the one
who didn't want them, not really.
You must remember the salty crashing of your own
blood.

Let the carrion-eater masticate on wings of your old
friends. Dead friends.

Dead friends tell no lies.

The field is a massacre
and there's a knife inside your flaking cocoon.

What have you done?

I am here to show you how to scream with your skin off.

BY THE THROAT

J. Danielle Dorn

Another cloudy evening in a city with no stars.

Sandra knows where to look to find the moon even in the light pollution. Every evening she pulls aside the curtain in the living room before leaving her apartment and takes a quick glance skyward. Tonight, Sandra doesn't see the big fat glow of the only moon phase normal folks recognize.

Half. Waxing.

Good, Sandra thinks.

She wants to wish the moon were waning, the thinning of visible light a good omen for half-bloods like her. Or her father, who was only funny in private, when the others weren't around.

Wish in one hand shit in the other; see which one fills up first, her father used to say. Used to say a lot of things, before he died.

She checks the moon before she checks the weather. Routine. Check the sky, check her pockets, check her boots. Her shift starts at 20:00 and ends at 08:00. Not quite dusk and not quite dawn. It took her a few weeks of being in the city, to learn to use a clock to tell time. Celestial bodies were not reliable.

People who had spent their life here, ask her why she left Vermont for, of all places, Boston. It's not a bad question, but Sandra can only laugh when she hears it. The angle of the question is different to hers. They can't imagine why anyone would want to come to Boston.

Boston was the furthest she had ever been in her life.

Lou asks the most. She indulges her more often than anyone. Sometimes she jokes about running out of petrol and deciding to stay where the car broke down. Deflecting, of course. Dad's sense of humor.

Outside now and checking shadows. Her breathing is slow, even. When she first arrived, the city freaked her out. The lack of absolute dark during the night. Squinting into light pollution just to spy the galaxy.

Where the sirens came from and, eventually, what they meant which is where the paramedic idea had come from. Emergencies were her specialty, she figured. Why not.

Every evening she has checked the shadows and every evening she has seen nothing, only the shadows of dangers her new friends warned her about. Things like raccoons, muggers, junkies looking for a warm doorway to sleep or sate their addictions in.

"I don't know why we call it 'a drug habit,'" Lou said, after a particularly rough call. "It's not like you have to work at getting addicted. All it really takes is the one time, right?"

***

The warnings brought fresh caution. Her nails were gnawed and ragged.

She had been good about soaking and moisturizing and not picking at the cuticles or shredding them between her teeth, like the last bits of meat from a chicken wing. Used to be she would track the days she didn't bite them, reward herself at the end of each moon cycle. Hard to make any habit stick. Breaking this one just meant stepping out the door for her shift.

The brighter the moon glows on the night of a full-blood's birth, the stronger the curse of change in them. The stronger the effect they had on normal people too. This is a fact she keeps to herself. No one would believe her if she told them what full-bloods were capable of doing.

Back home, Sandra was known for two things: No fear, and her ability to stitch gruesome battle wounds in reckless full-bloods without vomiting.

She gives 'home' as little thought as possible, but the feelings, the sensations, are more difficult to suppress. The tingle of a full-blood's proximity, a shameful arousal mingling with base human terror.

Tonight, when she steps outside, Sandra feels the hairs on her arms stand erect, a well of prey-fear opening in her stomach, erupting up her spine.

Tonight is not like other nights.

In a city where she does not know all of her neighbors' faces, that familiar, hometown feeling, almost sends her into a panic.

Sandra likes to think she is, if nothing else, practical and panic is just another wound to stitch.

She checks. Nothing in the shadows. Nothing behind the tree growing out of the sidewalk, the banged-up postbox, between the cars parked in the lot behind her building.

She stands still and she stares into the darkness, pulling her cardigan tighter around her ribs, fingering the keys in the front pocket.

If she has to she can retrieve her blade from its place in her boot.

Silver has no effect on her people, and they don't howl at the damn moon, either. But they are hard to kill, and they can move fast as a buffeting wind when they need to. And she thinks, when she cannot find the source of the shiver, that whoever it is either lives in one of the nearby buildings or is standing so still that the shadows have granted them temporary shelter.

"Fuck," she says, and throws herself into the flimsy safety of her car.

**

It's a typical shift, which is to say Sandra and her partner Lou fly across the city. One call to the next, washing their hands up to the elbow and scrounging for loose PPE after each patient is delivered. The bean counters at Public Safety can't seem to keep up with all the gloves and masks they go through in a shift. This is what they end up bitching about at the end of the night.

Gas station coffee in one hand and her keys in another, Sandra hoists herself out of her car and shuts the door with her hip. It's long past dawn, a haze somewhere between fog and rain climbing over the city.

She takes all of five steps and there it is again. A tingle. Her stomach flops between fear and attraction. It spreads over the skin, goose pimples all over. The evening's junk food threatens to come back up.

"Okay creeper," she says, loud enough for anyone in the alley or watching from a rooftop to hear, "I know you're there, come out before I come find you."

Her apartment building is nestled in a stretch of struggling businesses and dingy bars, none of them able to keep the parking lot full. Plenty of places to hide.

One of them is watching. She waits by her car, dead leaves and bits of lost gravel crunching beneath someone else's shoes. A shadow comes.

Reflex has Sandra turning, winding up and throwing before anything else. The cardboard cup sails as hard as she can throw it.

It's Caleb.

Her little brother, six-foot-two, sun-baked and sun-bleached. Leaner and bonier than the last time they saw each other.

She should have thrown her keys too. Or a fist. He wasn't close enough for her to throw a fist.

"Whoa!" Caleb's arms form a reflex-quick shield again the paper cup. It bops to the asphalt, rolls away to join the rest of the trash. Judging by the way the sound draws his eyes, glancing, that's the first he's aware she had hurled trash at him. Someone else will have to pick up. "It's me!"

"I know!" Sandra snarls. Anger was a shield. It could be a weapon. "Who else is with you?"

"That's why I'm here!"

"WHO ELSE?"

"I—"

She's close enough. She presses her palms against his ribs and shoves and Caleb scuffs his heels back. Not even a full step.

He always used to let her win when they would wrestle when they were younger. When she was shorter.

"What did I say?"

"This is important!"

"What did I say?!"

"To never come near you again, but Sandra this is—"

"I DON'T CARE."

The last time she saw him:

Middle of nowhere. Dead father. Grief you don't recover from.

Yanked out of her house, marched to the back of a pickup truck, and thrown in.

Blood soaks her knees, on her chest and neck when her brother exhales, when his heart beats. The heady presence of another behind her, the heavy thump of a leather doctor's bag into the truck bed. Her brother's brother. The kind only full-bloods can be.

"I told you." Caleb draws a breath to speak and she cuts it off. "You have no right to tell me what to do or how to live my life. You think you do, but you don't."

"Sandy—"

Another thump, just as heavy. Without thinking, she snatches it up. It's not what she thinks it is. She doesn't know what to think it is. It's the arm that used to hold her down during play fights, the arm that taught her how to aim a rifle. It's been torn off at the shoulder. The wound is ragged. Full-blood claws are made for meat.

"Do not call me Sandy. Ever."

The heat in her face threatens tears. She will not give in to tears. She will not. Tears create an opening. Caleb is persistent. Hard to convince. Hard to kill.

All their kind are hard to kill, but Caleb is a bitter exception.

Arms out, his brow creases. He wants to get mad. If Sandra were full-blood, he would have let himself get mad.

"Would you just let me explain?"

She had always been able to look one of them dead in the eye. One of the very few. It irks her that she has to take a step back, so she can with him.

That's when she notices the shiner. Someone threw a wild punch at his stupid face and all she can think is,

Good.

Well. That's not all.

'How did this happen?' A shrill question, her pubescent body still trying to conform to a new voice. She's read her old anatomy textbook twice, taken notes and highlighted them.

'Just fix him, Sandy!'

'I CAN'T!'

She threads the needle and cries into the wound, fingers spreading fur, needle piercing flesh.

'I can't,' she says each time she cinches a new loop, 'I can't I can't I can't.'

She says again, "I don't. Care."

Caleb is tendon and muscle. Strong arms, blunt knuckles. The sight of him in banged-up jeans and a t-shirt that fits him like a sack makes her want to pull at her left thumb's hangnail. She resists. Bloodying up her own hands won't make her feel any more in control.

He draws the breath he had abandoned earlier and levels an accusatory finger into the alleyway between her building and the new Vietnamese sandwich shop. She still hasn't gotten to try their bánh mì yet.

"You've got an orphan circling," he says. "Alright? We found him up in the mountains, but he took off. Thought he would go back to his folks, but he didn't. I followed him here. He's been camped outside your place since at least last night."

She can't stop the repulsed shiver that runs through her. Caleb isn't here to try and bring her home. Boston was the biggest city, the only city, within about two hundred miles of The Compound. She had thought it was far enough.

As much as she wants to not care, she can't afford it. "He's here? Now?"

A distant door opens, and the middle-aged man who cleans up the bar between last call and opening comes out carrying two black trash bags and a slump in his meaty shoulders. Sandra never sees him unless either she is early getting home, or he is late getting out. All he can manage of Caleb is a quick glance. It's all he needs. The man quickens his step and once the bag has thumped into the dumpster he gets the hell out of there.

The siblings clench their jaws until he is gone.

"Look," Sandra says, reading the expression on her brother's stupid puppy face, "You reek. Come inside, take a shower. I'm gonna do the same thing, and then I'm gonna go to bed. You do whatever you gotta do—"

This doesn't work. If anything, he looks more wound up.

"—but I gotta go to sleep. I work for a living. You ain't dragging me back to the compound like I'm one of your little mountain goats."

"The what?"

"The—" Sandra catches herself with a deep sigh. "Town, Caleb. I'm not going back there. This is where I live now."

"Alright," His hands come up, a sign of surrender in a

land where everyone and their baby owns a rifle. They vanish into his front pockets a moment after. "I didn't come for you anyway, Sand... Sandra. I'm here for him. He needs to come home."

Five seconds of sizing him up, and she can find no sign of deception in his face or his posture. *Half-moon calm,* Dad would have called it.

Sandra trusts horoscopes more.

"Fine," she sighs again. "You still need a shower. I mean it, Caleb. You smell like shit."

That gets a laugh. It's just enough for Sandra to think that means they've settled the matter, and she pulls out her apartment keys.

***

When she rises again in the evening, the only sign her brother had ever been there is a set of folded sheets on the couch and a note scrawled and slapped to the door: *Get better LOCKS, this door SUCKS. Love, C.*

She holds the note in one hand, her keys in the other, hesitating. The prey-feeling doesn't greet her when she steps outside. The orphan must be gone, and her brother with him. They had discussed it that morning, and for all his other faults, Caleb isn't a liar. At least, she has no reason to think he would lie.

Until she came to the city, Sandra had never heard anybody use the word 'should.' Things either are, or they aren't. And all Sandra can tell is that right now, they aren't.

Per usual, it takes her the same amount of time to drive from her apartment to the ambulance corps, and as per usual she parks her car and gets to the locker room before she checks her phone.

"Don't get scared."

Which, of course, startles her. The phone drops and she whirls around, heart hammering like rabbit feet against her sternum. She faces Lou, all five-foot, freckle-faced, ninety pounds of her, who wants to laugh but knows better. Lou still doesn't know why Sandra is so jumpy. They told HR about the relationship ages ago.

"Oh my god," Lou says, "I'm so sorry, I wanted to do the opposite of that."

Lou gets a fast, gratuitous hug. At shift change, they have neither privacy nor time to kiss the way they want to kiss. The door keeps opening and closing, and the whine of the hinges reminds Sandra she has to let go fast.

"Sorry," she says, "I've got my head up my ass tonight."

"Hey man, I'd be freaked too. He didn't even warn you he was coming?"

"He doesn't have a phone."

"Shit."

The first of the day shift starts pouring in, clomping steel toe boots and raucous voices. No more patients for any of them. Sandra decides to tell Lou the story once they're transplanted in the city's shift-worker bar.

"Is your roommate still deodorant-striking?" Sandra asks, just to change the subject. It works.

Not even five minutes after Lou has pulled their ambulance out of its assigned spot and aimed it towards the nearest, cheapest coffee does dispatch break through the radio chatter to summon them to the scene of an indescribable injury.

"Caller says it looked like a wolf," the dispatcher says.

"A wolf." Lou's tone isn't a question.

"Yep."

"In an alley."

"Yep."

"You still got 'em on the line?"

"They're three stories up watching it happen."

"Smart. Give me the address again?"

And he does. And it pulls the plug keeping the color in Sandra's face. It drains away, graying vision and muffled hearing following. Panic is looking for a way out, assaulting ribs and cushioning heart.

Even Lou does not know where Sandra lives. After-shift drinks that turn into fooling around, always ends up at Lou's place. Lou is focused on driving and it buys Sandra some time. She has to get her breathing under control, has to smooth over her expression.

Sandra does not want to see what would happen if human law enforcement found Caleb. Metaphorical torches, figurative pitchforks. Badges respond to even imaginary threats, and Caleb is very real.

"Oh, hell," Lou says once they're on scene, once they can see what they're dealing with.

It's far from the worst injury they've dealt with before. Motor vehicles and farm equipment and shotguns bought from neighborhood box stores make unrecognizable piles of meat out of loved ones every shift.

Sandra still recognizes him. She recognizes the wound. An undisciplined young-blood tends to use their teeth instead of their claws.

She goes to her knees in the pool coagulating beneath

her brother, his windpipe torn and his jugular still spurting. The connection to his heart is severed but the jugular doesn't know that.

"I can fix this," Sandra rummages the suture kit out of her jump bag. She doesn't have gloves on. Her face shield is already down.

"You... what? Sandra—"

"I can... I can fix this. It's okay. Caleb? Caleb!"

His eyes flutter. He exhales, sprays blood across her plastic face shield. Lou flinches. Sandra doesn't.

Rank and bitter, the salve she scoops from the banged-up old tobacco tin makes her fingers prickle. The skin on her left hand is chewed to hell, her knuckles are raw and angry, her nail beds shredded.

Caleb takes a ragged, hungry breath of air, his bare chest inflates under a rasping throat. As if transferred, Sandra's own lungs give out a cough. A laugh, with bitter rank relief.

His body begins to change. He begins to change. Muscles ripple, gaining bulk that defies medical expertise. Nails grow long and sharp, his hair to coarse fur, new deep breaths with inhuman lungs to accommodate the new flesh. He wears his own blood, too much of it. Wet and furious.

When he opens his eyes, Sandra knows she is done for. She traded her life for his.

"Sandra!" Lou has bass in her voice now. "What are you doing? He's—"

Fighting to breathe though the only thing keeping his head attached to his body is the stubborn bones comprising his cervical spine. His inhales can't reach his lungs. He's paler than the sidewalk not yet struck with blood.

He's going to be okay.

The salve wasn't magic. It was made of chewed-up tree bark and spring muck and blood. They have proper antiseptics and ointments in the world outside the compound where she grew up. She knows that now.

"He's going to be okay." She's calm. She's done this before. "Get back in the truck."

Lou, however.

"What?"

Hands clasp her arms, dragging her out of the truck and away.

"Let me go!"

She is a half-blood. She has no claws. The hands only tighten when her heels drag against the dirt. Her brother's gasping becomes the roar of a monster.

"You gotta trust me, Lou. Please get back in the truck. I'll… He's gonna be okay, but you can't be here when he comes back."

"I…"

She stops stitching. Just for a moment. Holds pressure on her brother's jugular and looks at Lou, a fire in her eyes that no doubt frightens the human woman.

"*Please*, Lou. And tell dispatch we don't need police, he's gonna sign an AMA waiver."

"… *What?*"

Something is stirring inside the body on the ground, and it's enough to put that prey-fear into Lou. For the first time, she heeds what Sandra says. Whatever is about to happen, she doesn't want to be here to see it.

"… Okay," Lou says, and takes a step back. She says it again, "Okay," and runs back to the ambulance.

As she returns to her work, Sandra starts to hum a tune. The soothing tune is for her brother as much as for herself, and the siren wailing in the distance does not come for them.

WHERE A WITCH GOES TO BURN

Eve Harms

Crows caw from a red, sun-dipped horizon
cords cut into my welted wrists, I'm bound
My sore arms, pulled around a pole,
I'm pelted by stones, and look down

Down from the pyre at twisting, dirty faces
yelling and spitting, the fools light the fire
Losing the cool breeze, banished by the heat,
flames crackle and bite, to the villager's spite

No screams, no struggle, I stay brave and still
flames engulf me, I speak a final spell
My form turns to ash, my soul survives,
searching for a sister, to give my power

I float in the wind, for centuries and miles
pulled to the East, until my long journey ends
My spirit lands in a loud, busy building,
Full of humans, and sewing machine sounds

Like a magnet, I'm pulled to a black garment,
adorned with many sacred symbols
My soul enters the fabric, making them magic,
I'm plastered with a label: "occult leggings"

I'm bought with a click, on an app for cheap things,
made for pennies, sold for dollars, overseas
I'm packed up, ready to fulfill my destiny,
ready to help a sister, another witch

The witch opens my box, and wears me with glee,
posing with pentagram candles, she takes a selfie
"New magic candles in my Etsy shop," she posts,
then takes me off and tosses me in a pile

EXTRA WEIGHT

Laurel Hightower

Pacing hallways and bedrooms late at night and far from the sleep she so desperately needs. She looks from child to child, two boys whose breathing has always been fixed on her, by her. No one listens, every doctor and nurse a fight. It's her accent maybe, thick Alabama that makes them think she can be dismissed. But she won't be. Her boys, their lungs, they're her responsibility. She braces for the fight each day, listens for the catch in their chests, and will never stop worrying, or laying a hand to check for the rise and fall. The dry crunch of crackers that keeps her company in the nighttime watch, and she is judged, this woman who is our sister. Whose heart and arms are wide enough for children who are not her own. Who knows that every day is a battle she is weary of fighting, but she will never goddamn stop, because they are all her babies.

***

Three a.m. watches when she thought the worry was done. Eyes closed, not staring at the ceiling, that would admit defeat. Bullets dodged, fifty caliber, and wondering when their number is up. Scar tissue, maybe, but his father died of lung cancer last year and no one knew until it was far too late. *Do you have a family history of cancer,* they ask, and before he can finish listing the occasions of cells gone mad they stop him, because the answer is yes. How many times can one family dance with death? Exhaustion, and the rush of fear, the knowledge of alone. What the fuck. *How* the fuck. Knowing everyone has a cross to bear, but Jesus, don't let this be his.

Riding down the elevator from the oncology floor that bloody fucking week in the gray time of not knowing. The woman with the IV stand, sad smile and squeezed hand to the man that rides with her.

"I'm sorry," the woman says. "For everything this is putting on you."

He declaims, and she sees her future in their lives. Or not. It's for someone else to say, but for fuck's sake, at least he's still ornery enough to drive the nurses crazy.

"You married him," snorts one, only halfway joking.

"I know," she thinks, among other things.

***

She heads into a war zone every day. No hazard pay, but the risks are high and her armor is flimsy. Masks and sanitizing wipes she buys herself because there's little more than shrugs and patronizing shoulder pats from the people who should know better. There was a time she thought adults knew what they were doing, that administrators took careful inventory and made thoughtful decisions. She knows now that she is the only thing standing between her students and the possibility of something very bad. Today it is disease, but yesterday it was bullets.

She has her own child at home, splits her time and

headspace between being the best mom, and the best teacher. No room left in there for just being her.

"Take it easy," they tell her. "You can't save the world."

Perhaps not, but neither can she stop trying.

***

I am woman. My femininity is based on the meager amounts I consume—barely enough to keep a bird alive is the encomium I seek. I am small, delicate, take up little space in your world. I am fragile and silent. When you ask me to read out loud it is a contest—who is meekest? Who must we ask the most stringently to speak up?

Because if I speak quietly, and you ask me, maybe I'll know you're listening.

***

Zoning out in the flickering blue light because what's the point in going to bed? She sees the beach on screen, the gathering of friends who live that kind of life. She feels the yearning for it, the memory that she could have been part of, maybe, all those years ago, if only she'd known how. To let go of the known and sample the unknown.

For a moment she thinks of the invitation she saw, a nighttime beach bonfire, and she wants to be wanted there. But that time in her life is gone; if it ever really existed. Because even then, she didn't know how to experience it. How to just go and trust. Always believing she had no safety net, never knowing where they lay.

Is she sorry? Maybe a little, when she sees the old picture, the one she thinks she must have taken because she's not in frame. Until one day she sees herself, barely a shadow in the background, invisible even to herself.

Could she have been different? Maybe. She could even wish it, but it seems like a betrayal of all it took to get her here.

And she is *here*. This is what it took to make her be here now, eyes mostly front instead of gazing in the distance at who she wants to be.

THE PARROT

Sonora Taylor

Charles always loved to watch Melinda sleep. He stared at her as she lay with her eyes closed. Her lips were pressed together, as if she were considering a dream. Her bangs hung over her forehead, and her chin-length hair was matted against her bloody neck.

Melinda wasn't sleeping anymore. She lay dead on a cold metal table. Her broken body hidden under a sheet. The coroner assured him he wouldn't want to see what the car had done to her below her neck.

"I'm sorry for the dried blood," the coroner said. His voice was timid, and he spoke as if eternally choked with apology. Charles looked up at him. The coroner's fingers were laced together and drumming against his knuckles. Timid and nervous. How was such a coward involved in a career handling the dead? He'd first met the man four years ago, when Melinda's parents had been killed by a drunk driver. He hadn't liked the man then, and he still didn't all these years later, when Melinda had macabrely followed in her parents' footsteps.

"I would've cleaned her up more," the coroner continued. "But—"

"But you had to call me in to identify her. I get it." Charles looked down once again at his dead wife. Her skin was already paler, her lips a little too dusty. He imagined if she touched her, she'd be ice cold. His fingers twitched at his side.

"Do you want a moment alone?" the coroner asked.

Charles stiffened his posture and clenched his fingers back into his palm. "No thank you, Mister…"

The coroner raised his eyebrows. "We've met before."

Charles's lip twitched, but he kept the sneer from crawling up his lip. "It was years ago, and my wife was grieving her parents."

"Right. Well, it's Damon."

Charles glared at Damon, who looked down at his fidgeting hands. "Damon," Charles said in a cool voice. "Thank you for calling me."

"Of course, Mr. Baker."

"I'll make arrangements with the funeral home tomorrow and have them call you."

"Of course."

Charles nodded once, then turned to leave.

"Mr. Baker?"

Charles stopped, closed his eyes, and took a deep breath. He had to keep his patience in front of the coroner. He couldn't lose control in front of him. He turned, slowly, and locked eyes with Damon. Damon himself had bangs like Melinda. They hung in strings over eyes that seemed better suited for a puppy that constantly pissed itself than for a grown man.

"Yes?" Charles asked.

Damon swallowed. "Do you … we have pamphlets, you know. About grieving, and loss, and—"

"I know how to mourn my wife."

"Yes." Damon nodded as he clasped his hands. They finally stilled. "Of course."

If Charles heard Damon say "of course" one more

time, he was going to add another body to the table in the room. Charles gave a quick nod. "Good night, Damon."

"Good night."

Charles sped out of the coroner's office and out into the cold. He reached his car, then sat inside without turning on the engine. Dead. Melinda, his wife for the past four years, dead on a coroner's table. Struck by a car while walking home. Her body broken, her skin bloody, her head now devoid of dreams. Melinda was dead.

Charles gripped his steering wheel. *That fucking bitch.*

***

Melinda had the unfortunate quality of being able to elude Charles. When they first started dating, he saw her steadfast clinging to her own opinions as a challenge. The women before her had been like dogs, simpering creatures that cowered in his presence and cuddled to him so long as he fed them. Melinda was a cat, one who could scamper and scratch when she didn't want her master to do something to her. But cats were still pets, and Charles's greatest pleasure was domesticating his most elusive possession.

She'd had her moments, of course. Melinda dove deep into computer code, working in web design and app development with the intensity of an archeologist piecing together dinosaur bones. Melinda would get so involved in her work that Charles would come in and unplug her computer to get her attention. She'd screamed at him the first time he did that, and a smack across her face made her know better than to do that. She also learned not to get so lost that she'd neglect him. Melinda was a learner, but all he cared about her knowing was that as long as he was alive, he was her husband; and he would come first.

Yet that night, Melinda had eluded him in a way he couldn't correct. Charles clenched his teeth as he unlocked his front door. He wouldn't be surprised if she'd intentionally walked in front of that car. How dare she leave him like this? How could she leave him alone, after all he'd done to take care of her? To improve her as a woman, to make her perfect by making her his?

"Hello, Charles."

Charles jumped when he walked inside. He looked in the empty house, then collected himself. No one was there except for Melinda's Parrot.

The Parrot was a home device that, while once a product of Google or Amazon or one of those companies, Melinda had made her own. She'd spent hours tinkering with it in her office, modifying it to respond to unique commands and give unique answers. It turned on the television, set the house under an alarm that automatically turned off when it detected their keys, shared the weather, and more. Charles didn't mess with it too much, unless it was playing Melinda's music too loudly and he wanted it to turn the volume down.

Tonight, the Parrot glowed from its spot on the nightstand. It pulsed like a heartbeat, waiting for a command.

"Off," Charles said.

The Parrot dimmed into darkness. Charles sighed and walked up to his room. He'd deal with the funeral home tomorrow.

***

Charles woke up the next morning and reached for Melinda. The memory of her dead on the coroner's table entered his mind just before he touched her cold pillow. He groaned as he got out of bed. He'd have to make his own breakfast now. He wondered how long he'd need to wait before he could start dating again and not raise judgment. He put on his robe and walked down the stairs.

"Good morning, Charles."

Charles looked at the Parrot with weary eyes. Melinda had done some kind of scanning trick to enable the Parrot to scan a person and call them by name. It was useful in case of intruders—if it detected someone not in the system and without Charles or Melinda, it called the police—but it made it creepy when he was alone and a machine without eyes called him by name.

"Morning," Charles mumbled as he went into the kitchen.

"I have news for you today."

Charles heard the TV flick on and the familiar hum of their Roku booting up. Charles rolled his eyes as he turned on the coffee machine. "Can the news wait?" Charles asked as he walked into the living room.

"Here is the latest from CNN."

A video came on about the upcoming election. Charles sighed and made a mental note to change the settings when he was more awake. He returned to the kitchen while the news droned on in the living room. He poured himself a cup of coffee and a bowl of cereal, then returned to the living room.

"And here is news from FOX 5."

A video appeared, and a man with sandy hair and Cabbage Patch cheeks looked solemnly at the screen. "In sadder news, police have discovered the body of a man who went missing last month," the reporter said. "Zach Smith, 35, was found dead in the woods just outside of Fairfax. An autopsy will be performed, but the body shows signs of blunt trauma and choking."

"Turn this off," Charles commanded. He'd seen enough dead bodies the night before.

The Parrot didn't listen. Charles grabbed the remote, and the reporter continued. "The autopsy will be performed in the coming days. In other news, the 2012 election is heating up!"

Charles's thumb froze over the remote. 2012? Charles glanced at the wall calendar by the door, even though he knew it was 2016.

Charles turned off the TV and glanced at the Parrot. It glowed its green beam.

"Why did you show me an old news clip?" Charles asked, though mostly to himself.

"Today it will be fifty degrees," the Parrot replied. "Sunny but breezy."

Damn thing was busted. He'd get Melinda to fix it. Charles closed his eyes when he once again remembered that Melinda was dead.

"Where is Melinda?" the Parrot asked.

Another customization. If the Parrot didn't detect either of them for a period of time, it asked about them. Charles found it useful in making sure Melinda wasn't gone for long periods of time. He was pleasantly surprised she'd agreed to the change. She wasn't perfect, but she had her moments.

"Where is Melinda?" the Parrot asked again.

Charles swallowed. "Dead," he replied.

The Parrot pulsed in silence. Charles wondered if devices could mourn their creators.

"I'm going to work," Charles said as he moved to get his coat.

"Goodbye, Charles," the Parrot said.

**

Charles balanced office work with discreet calls to the funeral home. He didn't tell his coworkers that he was now a widower. He didn't think it was any of their business, and he didn't want them to try and send him home for bereavement leave. Melinda didn't have control over him in life, and he'd be damned if she influenced him while rotting in the downtown morgue.

He settled for cremation, which the morgue promised would be done by the following afternoon. He'd save arrangements with their lawyer and with financial advisors for later. Charles thanked his lucky stars that Melinda's parents were dead. He wouldn't have to call them, and he wouldn't have to fight with them over funeral arrangements or what to do with the body. There was no one else to meddle in their marriage, which was one of the many things that made it perfect.

Charles drove home that evening through skies that deepened further into indigo and violet as October stretched on. He walked inside with a sigh. It had been a long day, and though he'd come home from many a long day to find Melinda ignoring him while she meddled with code, there was a part of him that missed her presence all the same.

"Hello, Charles."

"Hello, Parrot." Charles realized the Parrot had never been given a cute name, like Siri or Alexa. Maybe he'd name it Melinda. He smirked. Finally, something named Melinda that listened to his every command.

"I have news for you today."

Charles furrowed his brow. "It's not morning."

The TV turned on and the Roku hummed to life. "Parrot, I don't need the news," Charles said.

"Here is news from NBC 4."

An attractive Black woman in a red blazer stared at Charles from the screen. "In other news, officials have found the body of a man who went missing six months ago. Dustin Wood, 37, was found in the Shenandoah Mountains after weeks of searching. His body showed signs of blunt trauma and choking."

Charles stood frozen as the news played out. Another murder from the past. "Parrot, only show me current news," Charles said.

The video stopped, and the Roku turned off. Charles sighed with relief. Finally, he'd been listened to.

"Where is Melinda?"

Charles closed his eyes. "I told you: She's dead."

"When will Melinda return?"

"Never."

"Do you know where Melinda is?"

"At the morgue!" Charles spun to face the Parrot, which glowed from the table. "At Westover Morgue and Crematorium, where she's going to be burned to ashes. So stop fucking asking about her!"

"Calling Westover Morgue and Crematorium."

Charles screamed into his fists as the sound of numbers dialing rang through the living room. "Cancel call!" he shouted.

The dialing stopped. The Parrot glowed but sat in silence.

Charles calmed enough to notice his stomach growl.

"Parrot, order pizza from Dominos," Charles commanded.

***

"Good morning, Charles."

Charles rubbed his eyes and ignored the Parrot. He'd had nightmares about the videos the Parrot had shown him the day before. He hoped that by not acknowledging it, it wouldn't play any more outdated clips.

"I have news for you."

Charles sighed as the Roku and television turned on. "What is it this time?" he grumbled.

"Here is news from ABC 7."

A video clip began, and Charles's eyes went wide. The reporter onscreen had left the station in 2015.

"In sad news today, an area man believed missing was found near the Potomac River—"

"Turn it off," Charles commanded.

The video paused on the moment where a man's picture appeared on the screen. A man who was now dead smiled at him.

"Let me guess: blunt trauma and choking?" Charles asked.

"Yes," the Parrot replied.

Charles narrowed his eyes at the Parrot. "You know

what's in all these clips?"

"They're for you, Charles."

Charles tried not to shudder. The Parrot just meant the news was for him, not the old videos. Damn thing was broken, and Melinda wasn't there to fix it.

Charles decided to get breakfast on the way to work. He grabbed his coat from the hook.

"Where is Melinda?"

"Dead," Charles snapped.

"Is she?"

Charles paused. "Yes," he said, more coolly this time.

"I'm sure you hope she is."

Charles looked at the Parrot. It wasn't glowing. Its green light shone in a static ring.

"I'm going to work," Charles said, with a stammer he hoped was slight enough for the Parrot not to detect.

"Goodbye, Charles." The Parrot's light stayed on. Charles watched, waiting for it to dim. After a few moments, he turned and sped out the door.

***

Charles's day was utter shit. Everyone at work seemed to be up his ass about something. Where was this report? When can we have this meeting? Couldn't they give him a break?

The only saving grace was leaving early to pick up Melinda's ashes. Charles left the funeral home with the urn in his hands and sped to his car so quickly that he almost ran into someone on the sidewalk.

"Mr. Baker!"

Charles looked up and saw Damon's punchable face.

"What do you want?" Charles snapped.

"Nothing. You almost collided into me—"

"I fucking know." He held up the urn. "I'm sorry I didn't notice you while carrying my dead wife."

"I'm sorry," Damon said, and Charles almost hated his acquiescence more than his insensitivity. Be a man, for Christ's sake.

"I know the woman who owns the funeral home," Damon added. "Amy. I told her to take good care of your wife."

"Well, it's a fine piece of metal," Charles said as he tapped the outside of the urn. "Good night."

He drove home with Melinda in the passenger seat beside him. He glanced at the urn and remembered the Parrot malfunctioning that morning, asking him if Melinda was dead. "You bet your digital ass she is," Charles said as he turned into his driveway.

He walked into his house with the urn cradled in his arm. "Hello, Charles," the Parrot chimed.

"Hello, Parrot."

"Where is Melinda?"

Right to the chase—but Charles didn't mind at all. He grinned and thunked the urn down next to the Parrot. "Right here."

A small green light scanned the urn from top to bottom. "Melinda's not here," the Parrot said.

"What's left of her is." Charles plopped onto the sofa and kicked off his shoes. "I've told you a thousand times: she's dead."

The Parrot, at last, sat in silence. Charles leaned back with a triumphant grin. "Parrot, turn on Netflix," he said. He was done thinking of Melinda for the day.

The TV turned on. A video was already paused onscreen. Charles wondered when the Roku had turned on. "Parrot, Netflix," Charles repeated.

The video began to play. It was shaky footage of the woods at night. Melinda walked through them with a flashlight bobbing back and forth beside her. Charles's eyes widened at the sight of her, vivacious and smiling.

"Isn't this perfect?" she said with a grin on her face. "I love the woods at night." She lifted the hand that held the flashlight to her mouth and did a whooping noise into the trees.

"Ssh," the person recording said.

Melinda laughed, and Charles sneered. "Parrot, what is this?" he asked.

The Parrot stayed frozen. Of course it was broken. Charles moved to grab it, when Melinda jerked her other hand upward. Charles froze when he saw what she held: a crying, quivering man who looked oddly familiar.

"There's no one else here," Melinda said. "Except this asshole."

"Help!" the man screamed.

A mallet swung from the point of view of the camera and struck the man in the chest. He dropped and gasped for breath. Melinda pulled something from the pocket of her hoodie and wrapped it around the man's neck, lifting his face to the camera.

"Smile!" she said.

The man's eyes bulged as he sputtered for breath. Charles recognized him facing frontward: he was Zach Smith, the murder victim that the Parrot had shown him the other day.

Charles' skin grew cold. The video turned off, and

Charles moved to turn off the Parrot with a trembling hand.

"I have news for you," the Parrot chimed.

Charles whipped his hand back. The TV flicked on again.

He was less surprised by the images on his screen, but no less horrified. Melinda held another man he'd seen the other day, Dustin Wood; with a cord wrapped around his throat. He had bruises on his skin and blood on his shirt.

"Give him another whack," Melinda said to the person holding the camera. "While he can feel it."

The camera was set down and stayed steady as Melinda's accomplice entered the frame. Charles gripped the couch cushions as Damon walked towards Dustin. He crashed the mallet down on Dustin's leg. Dustin let out a garbled scream.

Charles grabbed his cellphone. He had no clue where Melinda was, but Damon's ass was probably at the mortuary. He'd call the police.

The video cut to the mortuary. Melinda lay on the table as she'd done when Charles went to see her, when he'd been told she was dead. Her eyes were closed, but there was a smile on her face as she gasped for breath. Damon had his head between her thighs and his twitchy fingers clasped around her hips. Charles's blood boiled as Melinda cried out in ecstasy. Her head lolled to face the camera.

Fuck calling the police. Charles would kill the fucker himself. Charles jumped to his feet but stopped when a new video began. Melinda sat beside the dead body of another man, presumably the one they'd found in the Potomac River.

"Why'd you kill him?" Damon asked from behind the camera.

Melinda chuckled, then stroked the man's hair. She smiled her sexiest smile, one that in spite of himself, Charles remembered fondly. She looked straight into the camera, making eye contact with him.

"I killed him because I was practicing for you, Charles."

Charles stood frozen. His sneer vanished.

"I killed him and the others because I want to get it right when we finally come for you."

The video and TV cut off—as did all the lights. The Parrot darkened, then dimmed back on in battery mode. Its green glow was the only light left.

A key turned in the lock, and he heard the front door open. Charles stood still in the dark. Melinda was back. He'd show her. He'd wait in silence on the couch, wait for her to go upstairs or into the kitchen and then take care of her.

The Parrot glowed beside him. "Hello, Damon."

Charles's brow furrowed, but before he could turn, he felt something cold and hard smack against his head.

***

Charles opened his eyes and saw blurred shapes. The shapes sharpened into a desk chair, a desk, and Melinda's computer. Her computer stayed off. Damon sat in the chair, thumping his mallet up and down into his palm. "Hey there, sleepy," he said with a smile.

"Fuck you," Charles growled. He'd been out of it for who knew how long, but he remembered the hellish videos the Parrot had shown him clear as day—especially the way Damon had been eating out his wife.

"I'd rather fuck Melinda."

Charles tried to scramble to his feet but ended up scooting to no avail. He felt cords wrapped around his wrists.

"Tight little fuckers, aren't they?"

Charles looked up at the sound of Melinda's voice. "Where is she?" he spat.

A cord tightened around his neck. Charles gasped, then coughed. He thrashed and butted his head, until Damon rose and struck him on both ankles. "Thrashing makes it worse," he said.

"Listen to Damon." Melinda crouched in front of Charles. Her hair brushed his cheek as she descended, and she wore the perfume he'd once told her was his least favorite. He'd made his point by dumping it down the toilet. She held two long ends of cord in her hands, and Charles realized that it was the power cord to her computer.

Melinda grinned, then snapped her hands back. Charles flipped onto his back, and his scream was cut short as the cord around his neck tightened.

"I married the wrong man, Charles," she said. "But you married the wrong woman."

A flash of green caught Charles's attention. The Parrot sat on the bookshelf against the wall. "Hello, Melinda," it chimed.

"Parrot!" Charles called in a strangled voice, one growing weak in time with both his vision and breath.

"Hello, Charles," it replied.

Damon swung the mallet and struck Charles's chest.

He sputtered and coughed, but managed to choke out, "Parrot, call nine one one!"

Damon swiveled to face the Parrot with his mallet. "Damon, don't!" Melinda said as she tightened the cord. "It'll be fine."

Charles smirked as his vision blurred. Melinda and her precious tech. She'd been obsessed with her computer all throughout their marriage, and now she was shirking both Damon and their safety in favor of a damn home device. They were both fools.

"Hello, Charles," the Parrot repeated.

"Call nine one one!" Charles croaked.

"I have news for you."

"Jesus Christ! Call—"

"You're going to die."

Both Melinda and Damon laughed. Charles sagged to the floor as the power cord squeezed out his final breaths.

THE SILENCE OF SARAH CROSS

Beverley Lee

Sarah Cross placed her china cup upon the saucer, her fingers white-knuckled around the delicate handle. All eyes in the room had swung to her and she could feel their disapproval and shock settling on her skin.

'I'm sure Sarah didn't quite mean what she said. Perhaps a little air?' The words from her mother-in-law, Constance, rang out in the uncomfortable silence. But Sarah knew their true meaning from the glance Constance gave to the man standing by the hearth, a glass of brandy cupped in his palm. Her husband, Hugo.

'Of course.' Hugo strode across the room and placed his hand under her elbow. 'Come, my dear, let us retire to the balcony for a few moments. You are not yourself.'

Sarah had never felt more like herself than when she had uttered the words that had shocked the room's occupants.

In my opinion, girls should have the same opportunities as boys.

She wasn't sure which part of her speech had shocked the most. Women were not allowed an opinion, even though one of them sat upon the throne of the British Empire.

Hugo guided her, not to the balcony, but to the door leading to the entrance hall.

'You will go to your room,' he hissed against her ear.

'Before you embarrass me further.'

It had always been the same, ever since she was a girl. Decisions made about her future. Her education. Her marriage to an 'enviable match.' Her status in this Victorian society that prided itself as being forward thinking.

Children should be seen and not heard was a proverb from the fifteenth century. Written by a man, of course. But it may as well apply to women.

Her cheeks burned with the embarrassment of dismissal and she knew Hugo would have more to say later. The words that fell from his tongue could cut like a whiplash.

She ascended the marble staircase, one gloved hand trailing along the polished handrail, and felt the weight of all the years she had travelled and those yet to come.

The drapes had not been drawn in her room and she smiled. Maisie knew how much she loved to gaze out of the window, to imagine other lives, other ways to live.

The winter night was still, the cold light of an almost full moon casting cloud-shadows upon the frost-tipped cobbles.

She had always loved to be alone, had been frustrated at the people around her who equated alone with loneliness when it is not the same thing at all.

She swept her gaze across the chimney pots to the dark shoulder of the distant hill, to the sentinel silhouettes of the wind-battered pines. How she longed to climb this hill. How she longed to rid herself of corset and crinoline, to feel the wind tangling in her loose, dark hair.

In her peripheral vision she thought she saw something moving in the deep shadows along the rooftops but as she focused her gaze a soft rap sounded on her bedroom door and Maisie entered to turn down her sheets.

'Pardon me, Ma'am, but this came for you. I was told to bring it straight to your hand.'

Even in the soft glow of the candlelight Sarah could see the heightened colour on the young maid's cheeks, as though she were breaking a rule by not delivering it to Hugo.

Sarah took the small scrap of folded paper, curled her fingers around the damp parchment. She wanted to press Maisie more, but she was desperate to read whatever words were meant just for her.

As the maid's footsteps echoed down the hallway, Sarah unfolded the paper. Only three words were printed upon it.

I am listening.

Sleep remained elusive. She went to the window. In the parchment-coloured glow of the gas lamp stood a man, one hand resting upon a walking cane, and the wind, as it tunnelled down the narrow cobbled street, played in the folds of his cloak. Tantalising glimpses of crimson silk billowed in the overhead glow.

He opened one gloved hand. An identical scrap of paper to the one resting under her pillow slip rose into the air and was carried by the wind into the shadows. He raised his head, sweeping his top hat from his head in one fluid motion. A glimpse of a pale face, sharp eyes pin-pointing her in place, and long fair hair falling to his shoulders.

She stumbled backwards, collapsed heavily onto the cushions of a chaise longue, her fingertips pressed to her lips.

When she gained the courage to look again, the stranger had gone.

But he had left his mark upon her.

I am listening. The words he had written a Pied Piper call to her trampled soul.

She began to look forward to the fall of darkness, tried to stop the smile playing on her lips when her husband informed her he was taking the carriage into the city for business.

The stranger did not appear every night. It was as if he was testing her resolve. She began to yearn for his silent presence under the flickering gas light, and, as she waited, a shawl clutched around her shoulders, she began to think about the remainder of her life.

In the staid and monotonous days that followed she found her thoughts straying to these moonlight encounters, and she scolded herself for such frivolous thoughts. But the truth was that this was hers. She had not had it forced upon her by society or an overbearing husband.

A month after the first appearance of the man she once again peered around the curtain, her gaze fixed upon the circle of light from the gas lamp. But the stranger was not there.

He was standing by the gate, gloved hands curled around the fleur-de-lis tipped railings. He raised one hand and beckoned to her.

Heat rose to her cheeks and in the pit of her stomach butterflies took flight. But this time she did not back away.

The sash window was slightly open, and a scent drifted through the small gap. A rich, deep loam and something very green, like wet moss upon a gravestone.

She shivered but found the feeling strangely appealing.

'Sarah, come down to the gate and let me explain my intrusion into your life.'

His voice was soft but every syllable beautifully enunciated. The familiarity in which he addressed her should have given her cause for great concern but instead it had the opposite effect.

What harm could it do, she asked herself, tamping down the voice inside that screamed of all the harms possible.

As if he sensed her turmoil he backed away, pointed to the archway between the two tall, brick houses.

'I will wait by the carriageway. Dress yourself warmly.'

And with that, he disappeared into the shadows.

She began to dress, struggling with the layers of undergarments Maisie normally so deftly tied. Standing in front of her wardrobe door she flicked through the rails of silks and velvets until her fingers found the soft, grey wool of the plainest dress she owned. It would not do to attract attention she reasoned, whilst all the time her common sense warred with the rapid beating of her heart.

This might not be proper in society's eyes, but it was what she wanted to do, and if it damned her, so be it. But she thought about her children, sleeping soundly in the nursery and the scale of guilt and duty balanced precariously in her mind.

Pulling on black ankle boots her fingers fumbled with the buttons. The rest of the household had retired, apart from the doorman who would await her husband's return from the city, and she knew he would be snoozing in the chair by the entrance hall hearth, half-listening for the sound of hooves on the cobblestones.

Her heartbeat thudded against her ears as she crept to the back of the house, taking the door which led to the servant's staircase to avoid being seen.

And with each step towards the darkness of the scullery and the cobblestones beyond, she began to feel a new spark of life igniting within her veins. If anyone had asked her, she could not have told them why, only that this was the first decision she had made for herself.

She lifted the latch, the metal cold against her fingers and stepped out into the shadows, knowing she could never explain why she was here if she was discovered.

The archway was as black as pitch. Her boots echoed on the slick cobbles. She trailed one hand along the wall to keep herself upright, but her heel caught in a depression between two of the stones and she stumbled. Before her knees could hit the ground, a strong hand gripped her elbow, guiding her to the entrance of the archway.

'Who are you?' she asked, as he dropped his hand.

'Names are simply markers, Sarah. I could give you mine, but how do you know that I speak the truth?'

His face was half hidden by the brim of his hat.

'Call me just a man here as a pointer, a signpost if you will,' he said softly. 'Know that I do not wish you any harm and any choices you make are entirely your own. I wish to speak with you, to hear your views on the world in which we live.'

She wanted to ask how he knew so much about her. How he *knew* her. But instead her tongue leapt to a conclusion she had been conditioned to accept.

'Do not mock me, Sir.'

'Mockery is for those who gain pleasure from belittling others, much like your husband. I assure you that I will never heap ridicule upon you.'

His words came with the offer of his arm. She took it, felt the chill from the damp cloth. How long had he waited at her window this night?

He led her along the deserted streets, keeping to the back alleys, and gradually she relaxed into his company as they discussed her views on the arts and politics, the state of the empire and the recent construction of the glass houses at Kew.

Genuine interest in her words shone in the brightness of his eyes, and he matched her opinions with his own until their speech became a melody and she was giddy with the relief of finally being heard.

Her breath fogged in the cold air and the silence of the mist-drenched cobbles became the stage for all of the words she had held inside for so many years.

'You are a remarkable woman, Sarah,' he said as they came to a narrow passageway between the looming side of a terrace of fine houses and the wall that surrounded the graveyard. 'And that is why I chose you.'

'Chose?' She paused, shrank back against the cold stones. The first stirrings of unease took flight in her stomach.

'Indeed,' he replied, his steps not faltering. 'Or maybe it was fate that led me to your window.' He looked over his shoulder, the tip of his cane tapping against the cobblestones. 'Come, Sarah. I want to show you something. And I will ask you a question that you do not need to answer until you have seen and understood.'

Her feet crossed the shadow of the wrought iron arch suspended over the passageway, and she felt in her bones that she had crossed not only under it but through a line she could not retreat from. And she found, much to her surprise, that she did not fear the outcome.

The stranger stood by the lychgate at the entrance to the graveyard. She knew the macabre history of the structure with the pitched wooden roof, knew that in days gone by the shroud-wrapped body of corpses would rest here awaiting the minister.

He led her through the lychgate to the pathway that curved past the weather-beaten stones of the Saxon church, past the ornate grave markers and stately tombs surrounded by chains and railings. Even in death some people flaunted their wealth.

He ducked under the low hanging branches of a crooked yew, his hand cupping a cluster of bright red berries.

'The yew is a tree of rebirth and regeneration. It teaches us not to fear death but to view it as a transformation. Nearly every churchyard has one. It is fitting, do you not think?'

His words had a lilt about them now, an accent she would have penned as French if she had heard him for the first time.

He was not who he seemed to be.

Who do I want him to be?

He continued to the rear of the churchyard, far away from the array of fine stones. A patch of disturbed earth yawned at his feet, a simple grave marker at one end.

The stranger shook his head, bending to take a handful of earth.

'Do you still wish to know my name?'

The accent was there again, this time more fluid, more natural. He was lapsing into his native state.

'If it would please you to tell me,' she said, as her boots sunk into the soft ground.

'Always so proper, Sarah. I admire that about you even though I know your inner turmoil.'

He swept off his cloak, laid it on the ground beside the disturbed soil. Motioned for her to kneel.

The sound of carriage wheels rumbled over the cobbles close by. A whinny from a horse and the sharp snap of leather reins as life continued normally.

'If you had a choice, would you change your life, even if it that choice caused you immeasurable pain?'

A fine mist fell from the midnight sky. She could taste the smoke from the nearby factory on her tongue as his words settled on her damp skin.

She shivered. It was as if he had opened a door to her innermost thoughts and stolen one away.

But this, this moment, as the stranger waited, poised unnaturally still, his features cast in shadows from the moonlight caught in the protective branches of the yew. This moment was another boundary line to cross.

She fell to her knees on the fine wool of his cloak, its scarlet interior spreading like blood across the damp earth.

He pointed to the words engraved upon the marker.

She leaned across, her fingers brushing away a tangle of ivy. Her brow furrowed. She could not understand why he wanted her to look.

Jean-Sebastien Freniere – 1707–1737

Her gaze swept from the marker to his face.

Engrained dirt marred the collar of his lace shirt and other stains blemished its front. The cloak had been a disguise, just like his cultured English accent.

'What are you?' she asked, a chill bleaching against her bones.

'Ah, at last, dear lady, you finally ask the right question.'

He offered her his hand as she knelt before him. Nodded as the realisation made the breath catch in her throat. A broad smile graced his face. His teeth were white. Two curved canines glinted in the dark.

'Yes,' she whispered, and as his chilled lips traced the column of her throat, she waited for the pain of fang rending flesh.

And when it came it was as if she was tethered not only to him but to another world edged in crimson silk.

He pressed his sliced wrist against her lips. Her tongue flicked out. The first droplet of blood burst through the haze of pain threading through her veins. She grabbed his wrist with both hands and latched onto the wound like a starving newborn as he rocked her in his arms.

Sarah Cross was both lost and found.

***

It was easy to climb the trellis clinging to the wall. Rose petals floated to the ground as her fingers curled under the sash window.

The room beyond was in total darkness, apart from a sliver of moonlight that carved the bed in two.

Her upper lip curled as the smell of shaving foam and

stale cologne assaulted her senses. The richness of his blood oozed through his pores as he slept. But it was not this she had come for.

Her feet touched down on the floorboards she used to walk upon, and her shadow crept over the sleeping form of Hugo Cross.

Age had made his body softer and his once jet-black hair was threaded with silver.

He stirred slightly, and she cocked her head to one side as though she were a bird studying a worm.

Was it revenge she had come for? She had asked herself that question many times. Not revenge, but a need to make a point.

She settled upon the silk coverlet, let her fingers play across its cool surface.

'Hugo.' His name left her lips.

His eyes flew open, an intake of breath rattling in his throat. Her hand came down across his mouth, and she could feel his spittle against her palm. He did not expect the strength of her grasp, and he certainly did not expect her fang-tipped smile.

She had played this moment over and over in her thoughts. How would she complete her deed? But as he struggled under her unyielding grip the answer came unbidden.

She unclamped her hand from his mouth, saw his trembling lips open and heard the gasp which would come before his scream.

And in that instant her fingers dove into his mouth, clasping his tongue. This tongue that had spoken for her so many times. This tongue that had silenced any of her own.

Her fingernails sank into its wet softness and he arched underneath her, his hands flaying at her chest.

'Remember me, Hugo,' she whispered.

And then she twisted her wrist and yanked her arm back sharply.

A gargle came from his throat as dark blood spilled over his lips, staining the white sheets scarlet. He tried to speak but the muscular organ that had enabled him to do this lay in her fist.

She wanted to feel triumphant, but the feeling that washed over her as she slipped out into the night was one of closure.

***

And now she stood on the hillside overlooking the town where she had used to live. She could see the church tower through the trees, could imagine exactly how it looked in the dark.

Shortly, she would go down and walk the narrow pathways to the grave of Jean-Sebastien Freniere, even though she knew he did not lay beneath the cold earth.

Vampire. A name found in penny dreadfuls and a recent literature publication from Bram Stoker. A smile quirked her lips.

She had made a choice on that night as the soft mist fell, one she could never retreat from.

A second chance to be what she wanted to be. To achieve everything that had been denied.

And yes, it had come with a deep blanket of sadness.

She watched her children grow, had to stem the ache in her chest when life did not treat them fairly. Watched them die.

Her gaze lifts again to the hillside, to the still form she knows is watching. Her maker. Her liberator.

Some nights she takes him to her bed, but always on her terms.

More often she roams the rolling moorland with the swell of the sea at her back. At one with the darkness that conceals and protects her, the song of the blood in her veins.

Her hand strays to the leather thong resting on her breast. To the curled husk of flesh tied upon it.

She had been told her words counted for nothing.

Now she wore her husband's tongue as a reminder never to be silenced again.

As a cloud passed over the face of the watching moon, she threw back her head and howled, her right to exist echoing on the wind.

LOBSTER TRAP

V. Castro

The waters surrounding the islands are cold and rocky. Below the surface the darkness overtakes the light. Thick sashes of seaweed dance with the tide and patches of sea grass float like mermaid's hair clinging to the sea floor and feet of the cliffs. Bathers rarely venture far, even if they did, we would never harm them if they left us alone. A silent respect. The only ones who dare are the fishermen. Greed is bold. Arrogance is fearless. We now know they set their traps in no set pattern to confuse us at the midpoint between the shallows and a deep-sea floor ridge. Many of us were lost until we understood what they were doing. The further out we moved, the further they pursued us despite the ocean being filled with fish in the thousands. The land blossoming with other means of sustenance.

Their only goal is to trap at least one of my sisters at a time. And it is not out of hunger. Oh no, it is sport, ritual. We are as large as the fisherman, sight and mouths evolved more like their species than the smaller version of us. We do not know who first declared us a delicacy, a sweet meat to be consumed. Trophy.

It first happened in a tide of confusion, the stormy weather making the waters tumble with natural vitriol. We noticed one of us missing. As our eyes searched, flashing images of the ocean bounced in our collective sight. Antennas outstretched and swayed violently as we searched. Then we saw her in a knitted box. She struggled in confusion. Her mighty claws hitting the sides to find a weak point to escape. We could hear her wailing in our single consciousness.

Escape. Let me Out. I'm scared.

We rushed through the water as fast as we could before seeing the box rising from the waters with her trapped inside. We couldn't get to her, help her. We remained helpless as she disappeared into the air as a dark silhouette against the sunlight.

Eventually the waters calmed. Until another one of us disappeared in all the same way. None of us ventured far alone afraid of finding one in our path. We learned to live with this fear like the constant sound of the sea trapped inside of a conch shell. It became maddening for all of us. A tight net around our consciousness. Something had to be done. This was not a natural state of existence. We had not evolved any defenses for this predator. Our claws and teeth meant for the creatures down here. After the last disappearance, I took it upon myself to see what happened after we are taken from our habitat. My sisters would wait and watch in our collective vision in our nest in one of the underwater coves carved in the feet of the cliffs. I climbed the sloping rocks not far from the long piece of driftwood where they tie their floating vessels. The last of the sunlight in the sky would help me see. But we evolved with heightened senses to survive. I knew I could hide in the shadows. They never ventured out as the sun fell into the horizon. My antennas that hold two of my eyes rose from the water, leaving most of my body still covered.

On the driftwood they took turns inspecting and prodding our sister clinging to life outside of water.

Bubbles and foam oozed from her mouth. Her long, segmented tail flapped against their legs. She wanted to be cast back to the place she belongs, free. Their smiling sunburned faces laughed with each other. Their skin peeling like scraped fish scales. Unlike us, their bodies are soft. As soft as an urchin without a shell. A cave with driftwood walls as white as a pearl stands in the distance with a spike jutting to the sky.

A large clam shell that is not a clam shell stands where the sand meets soil. Heat, like vents at the ocean floor burns beneath it. A group of them spill out of the white cave made from driftwood as it opens. They gather around to watch my writhing sister be pulled towards the round hot boiling thing. Something like braided seaweed is wrapped around her tail. She is lifted into the air by a large object, made from the material they make their boats. Then she is lowered into the boiling clam shell. Screaming. I want to look away, but I cannot. I have to know. I have to see.

Her screaming stops. She is taken out silent and blood red. Red like our eggs. They clap and cheer. The cold water that I usually do not feel invades my body.

She is cracked open from the bottom orifice, next at the tail where we store our eggs, to the top joint where our body meets our neck. Ten arms hang lifelessly, water and seaweed still clinging to her. They clink shiny objects and sing songs about the treasures of the sea while we weep for the ones we lost. Our screams and wails carried away by the constant murmur of the tides. Waves hitting rock.

I have seen enough and slip beneath the sea. I sink inside as my body moves in weightless sorrow to meet my sisters.

The seasons are changing. They will begin to catch as much as they can to keep for when the waters are too dangerous. We have a plan. They are not the only ones with thoughts and hearts. When the fog rolls in we will set our own trap. We curse the traps they set for us so they might stuff their bellies and grease their mouths. Make more of themselves to move across the coastline. We evolved at the depths of the water. The elders say we are drowned humans cast from the pearl colored driftwood cave. Mermaid magic gave us life again. Reborn and evolving to withstand time. Although the mermaids left long ago. My fear is they too became caught in traps. Perhaps some are left. I would like to find them one day. But whatever they may have done to us, even the sharks know to steer clear because we hunt in packs. If you see one of us, twenty more are waiting to attack. The fishermen are not the only ones with a cunning nature.

These fishermen are not natural, don't belong in the habitat below the water, yet they have claimed it and all its contents for their own. Even the largest of us cannot escape. You can smell burning whale blubber for days. No care if a calf is left without a mother.

The deep ridge is further out than they have ever set their own traps. Day by day we inch closer to the ridge. They pull up their traps in disappointment. The following day a little further. Once they are beyond the ridge we wait. As they retrieve their traps, we use our great bulk to pull in the opposite direction, deeper into the water beyond the ridge. Mouth to tail, pulling harder on the trap until their vessels capsize, releasing blood and guts they use to capture others into the water. As their soft bodies flail in the current, that is when the sharks move in. The waters beyond the ridge are dangerous, no one escapes. No one survives the jaws of Mako and Great White. The hammerheads gnashing wild with hunger. We crawl to the ridge and watch *them* become the delicacy. Their final moments in fear and panic as they are torn in different directions by the predators of the sea. Strings of flesh and sinew polluting the water. More come to feast until nothing is left.

Still they continue this little game. I wonder when they will ever learn. Perhaps when none of them are left we will be free again. My next plan is to venture to the coastline to find the last of the mermaids and their magic.

DOLL HOUSE

Red Lagoe

Allison didn't have to cut herself open to know she was pretty on the inside. All she ever wanted was for Mama to see it, but Mama had trouble seeing beauty. Cutting remarks about her appearance were far more common than expressions of love.

Looking like TV women is hard work, Mama said. They starved themselves to be skinny, much like Mama starved Allison. Down to half-portion meals twice a day. The *perfect* women had cosmetic work done, just like the dolls lining Allison's wall. Zip-tied in a box with unnaturally tiny waists and perky, pointy breasts. Downturned toes delicate like ballerinas.

Instead of affection, Mama gave Allison flawed dolls for her to meticulously carve. Using kitchen knives, razor blades, and melted candle wax, Allison had honed her doll-sculpting skills over the past year, transforming the misshapen things into replicas of the perky ones in the pink boxes from Mama's childhood.

Heavy footsteps marched overhead. Something dragged across the floorboards. The upstairs door opened, flooding the steps with a wash of daylight. Allison's heart vibrated beneath a dingy purple shirt—unicorn sparkles rubbed off long ago. Harsh fluorescent overheads failed to pick up the tiniest glint of remnant glitter.

A woman's body tumbled down the steps, knees over ears, and crashed to the cement floor.

"Got you another doll." Mama's broad shoulders eclipsed the light from the stairway as she came down the steps.

Allison helped her mom lift the woman from the cement onto a pallet in the center of the basement. In Allison's weakened state, her scrawny arms could barely lift a plate of food, let alone a body.

Sunken cheeks and eye sockets made her almost unrecognizable. Bony legs where there once was muscle. Mama said thighs can't touch, so she took away Allison's carbs. Sometimes, Allison would sneak upstairs, unlock the basement door with her pins and steal a slice of bread.

Sometimes she got jealous of Mama's birds because she'd throw them bits of the bread ends. When Allison was little, she used to feed them with her, but she didn't go outside anymore.

A long time ago, Mama caught Allison feeding a squirrel. She thought they were cute until Mama's toxic glare insisted otherwise.

"They're nothing but ugly rats," Mama had said, laying out poison.

Allison supposed they were a little rat-like. She had watched a medical show once depicting the dissection of a lab rat. Its tiny insides were delicately arranged. Curious if the squirrel was really like a rat on the inside, Allison got ahold of the sharpest kitchen knife she could find and sliced a dead squirrel down the abdomen. The pink, stringy sinew bloomed from the incision, exposing bone and a network of connective tissue. *Beautiful.*

But Mama hated it when Allison exposed the insides. She slapped her across the face after catching her the first time with that squirrel. Now, Allison would rather have animals again than the dolls Mama brought.

A baseball bat from her high school days knocked the victims out. She didn't call them victims, though. They were *almost dolls*, so close to being pretty. A concussion kept them still and an injection of antifreeze finished them off. Then Mama dragged them to the basement for Allison to *fix*.

A twenty-something woman lay on the red-stained basement pallet, wearing tattered jeans and a tee. Thick, dark hair bundled around the woman's face, round and rosy. Bruises appeared on her cheek bones from the blow to the face. Thin and tall with delicate curves.

Allison couldn't think of a single thing to change.

"What's wrong with her?" Allison asked.

"That freckle is disgusting."

A small brown mole on her cheek did create an asymmetry to her face.

"Her hips." Mama's upper lip curled. "The blow to the head killed her. No antifreeze this time."

Allison felt for a pulse, but there was nothing.

Mama pat Allison on the head and hurried back upstairs. The latch clicked.

The door locked for the first time last year. She cried to be let out of the dank dark, but Mama insisted it was the only way to protect her. If the police knew what she had done to Mrs. Brenniman, she'd be taken away. So Allison never screamed for help.

She inspected the woman on the table. Smooth skin. Pretty. Just a raised freckle beneath the right eye.

Mama called moles nasty. Fortunately for Allison, all her face freckles were flat. But sometimes she caught Mama's contempt-ridden eyes staring at her mottled face.

At the end of the pallet, sat a three-story doll house. She unfolded the walls to expose its interior layers. Atrophied arms struggled to pull it apart. Allison would need to steal more bread tonight or she'd waste away. She forced open the dollhouse—no longer for miniature people and furniture. It was a home for her tools. Various knives, razor blades, many too old and jagged to make a smooth incision.

A lit candle melted a pool of tan wax as Allison sifted through her straight-edge razor blades. Sliding tools out of the way, she dug for the best one—the only blade left that wasn't rusted. If all her tools all wore out, maybe Mama would stop bringing her dolls. It had been increasingly difficult to find flaws as Mama's standards approached impossible.

The option of learning something new crept into Allison's daily wishes. She was good at carving and cutting. Maybe she could use her skills for something else. Something *good*. If she learned how to fix bodies the way they're meant to be, rather than how Mama thought they should be, she could become a surgeon someday.

Doctor Allison, plastic surgeon. Or maybe even...*brain surgeon extraordinaire.*

"You look like a...Sara," she said. "Can I call you Sara?"

She pressed the blade to Sara's face, just below the raised freckle under her eye. The razor's edge depressed healthy skin and sliced through, releasing blood. She dragged it in a tight circle, skin tugging at the dull blade. Allison's hand trembled. Frail fingers could hardly hold the tool. Blood pooled at the incision and trickled down the cheek.

Sara moaned under the knife.

Allison jerked back, about to call for Mama, to let her know Sara was still alive, but she held her tongue. Mama often complained of the dolls' lackluster complexions. If she kept her alive, it wouldn't be a problem. This sculpture could be her best yet, and the doll wouldn't have to die.

The spongy mole sat pinched between Allison's feeble fingers, still attached to the woman's face. She focused her energy on steadying the razor blade. It wavered above Sara's face. Allison pulled the mole farther from the skin, attached only by a sinewy string of pink flesh.

Just a nick of the razor against that little flesh wire. The metal swiped beneath her pinched fingers and cut the mole loose. Tendon-like string snapped back to Sara's face.

Sara groaned, eyes twitching beneath heavy lids.

Allison dropped the mole to the floor and pulled duct tape from her house of tools. She strapped Sara to the pallet and went back to work.

Detailed smoothing, sculpting like a famous artist, Allison patched the bloody divot with a dab of wax.

Sara's twitching settled and Allison moved on. A perfect, slender neck. Collar bones a lovely shape. Arms strong, lean muscle. Allison sat beside her sculpture, too tired to think about anything but how desperately she needed to eat. But she had to find something to fix or Mama would be mad.

Her eyes drifted down Sara's arms, toward her hands. Veiny.

She'd never fixed blood vessels before. Severing

them would only cause pooling of blood under the skin and discoloration. Perhaps if she peeled back the skin, she could figure out what to do with the bulging veins. It was an excellent opportunity to learn a bit of anatomy too. *Doctor Allison—cardiovascular surgeon.*

She lifted the blade, then closed in on the back of Sara's hand. With precision, she cut into flesh. Blood spilled to the floor. From the wrist bone to pinky knuckle, she cut through all layers of skin. Concentrating on the blade's movements, Allison turned the worn tool ninety degrees for a trip across the knuckles. The razor snagged on tough skin. Metal dug down to bone, rising and falling with each mound of the knuckles. She turned another sharp corner back toward the wrist. A rectangular flap on the hand was ready to peel back. It required some strength, but Allison got a grip on the skin flap. A centimeter ripped back with each tug, freeing skin from underlying disuse. She revealed a delicate masterpiece of vessel, tendon, and bone.

Sara twitched as her raw flesh was exposed. Groggy eyes made contact with Allison's. She shifted, trying to sit up, but was taped securely to the pallet. The moment of realization appeared on Sara's face—that she was restrained. She winced and looked toward her hand where blood pooled in the grooves, between bones and spilled over.

When the women on the table weren't breathing, they were just dolls to Allison. But this one was *alive*, with thoughts and fears.

"Mama?" Allison called.

The woman let loose a shriek that dragged Allison out of doll play and into the gruesome reality. Sara's eyes darted around the room. A guttural roar tore up her throat and howled out.

It's not your fault, she wanted to say, but all that came out was, "I think you're pretty."

For the first time, Allison felt bad for the doll on her table. It wasn't fair she couldn't meet Mama's standards. With each of Sara's panicked breaths, rationality for all the senseless butchery waned in Allison's mind.

Sara's eyes scanned the room, settling on the bodies against the wall. Her eyes bulged at the sight. Four dolls hung in their upright, casket-sized boxes along the shadowy basement wall. Women who Mama said weren't pretty enough. Looking at them now, Allison could see how it might be terrifying for poor Sara.

The first was their old neighbor, Mrs. Brenniman. About a year ago, she caught Allison in the backyard with a dead crow on its back, internal organs arranged outside its body into the shape of a rose. A black-winged rose. The sunlight glistened off the moist folds of flesh like dew on petals. Mrs. Brenniman didn't scream. She covered her mouth and tried to back out of the yard, but Allison panicked. She ran to the gate and blocked her from leaving.

"Please don't tell my mama," she begged.

Mama ran out of the kitchen with a steak knife in her hand. A blur of a memory, Mama's hesitation as her eyes darted between the dead crow and Mrs. Brenniman. The knife slitting Mrs. Brenniman's throat. Her head cracking against the pavers. Scarlet poured out of her skull and throat, soaking into the porous stone patio. The memory was splotchy, but not the words Mama said. "Damn it, Allison. Now look what you did!"

"Why'd you kill her, Mama?"

"What if she told someone what you did to that bird?"

"It was already dead."

"I told you not to be cutting up animals. If anyone finds out how messed up you are, they'll take you away."

"But why'd you kill her?" The question had never been answered.

Instead, they cleaned the blood from the patio, then dragged Mrs. Brenniman to the basement.

"I'm sorry." Allison's tears soaked into her purple shirt. Fluorescent light lit up the sparkles like fireworks.

"She deserved it." Mama turned to Mrs. Brenniman's body. "You think you're so perfect." Tears dragged mascara down Mama's cheeks. "Well your breasts are too big." Mama pulled her steak knife from her apron pocket and cut through her dead neighbor's shirt, exposing her breasts. She stabbed through tissue, slashed out fat from the breasts. Then she moved on to the double chin which only existed in Mrs. Brenniman's current limp state. She sliced into it, digging out flesh and fat, severing vessels. Blood splattered on the walls, drenched the concrete floor, and soaked through Allison's clothes.

Mama came out of her knife-slashing frenzy and melted to the floor in a pool of Mrs. Brenniman's blood. "It's ugly! It's all so ugly!" She handed the knife over to Allison and left her alone in the basement to clean up the mess.

Mama had recklessly torn through the body. The insides were prettier than the mangled mess Mama left behind. Allison spent the afternoon sewing and wax-sealing Mrs. Brenniman, hoping to earn Mama's forgiveness. Hoping to make her pretty enough for Mama to look at. Mama approved of Allison's work…and brought her more bodies.

All four of the victims lined the wall. Organs removed to carve the tapered waistlines to be close to the spine. Breasts had been either downsized by slicing away tissue or enlarged and lifted with poly-fiber stuffing. Feet narrow and pointy—shaping bone was the hardest for Allison. Without a bone saw, she had to use serrated knifes to cut through. Hack-jobs, but wax helped sculpt a finished look. With Mama's help, all of the women were then zip-tied upright into locker-sized cubbies, painted pink like the pink boxes of Mama's childhood dolls. Tears filled her eyes with each one. "You're getting better," she'd say with a smile. "But not quite perfect."

Sara's screaming brought Mama charging downstairs with a baseball bat over her shoulder. "Why is she *alive*?"

"Mama, don't kill her—"

The bat swiped through the air so fast Allison's hair whipped across her face.

Sara's piercing screams echoed off the basement walls, fluttering around like wild birds. Mama's bat cracked against Sara's temple and the screams crashed into sudden silence.

Panting, Mama nodded toward Sara's hand. The skin was peeled back, blood drooling to the floor. "What the hell are you doing to her hand?"

"They were veiny." Saying it aloud, it sounded insane.

"What does *that* matter?" Mama rubbed the rolling veins of her own hand.

Allison hung her head.

She scanned her daughter and leaned in. "What's

that?" Her finger depressed into a soft lump on Allison's chest. Her face went sour, lips downturned. "Are those supposed to be breasts?"

"I don't know." Allison protected her chest with crossed arms.

Mama covered her mouth. "Your butt is getting bigger too." Her eyebrows arched, lips pursed. "And your face. You're getting fatter."

"I'm just growing."

"You're growing the wrong way. Better cut out your dairy now."

"I'm starving!"

Mama's poisonous gaze pierced through her. "Better than being ugly." She pointed to the corpse on the table. "Clean her up." The authoritative command of Mama's voice vibrated through her, screaming through veins, bouncing from bone to bone, insulting every bit as it skittered around.

Mama stormed up the stairs, leaving Allison alone with the dead. Sara lay on the table, skin pale blue, lifeless. Maybe it was all ugly. Allison twisted to get a look at her backside in the blood-splattered mirror. There wasn't much left of it, but she could see the bulge Mama thought was fat. And her breasts were just starting to come in. She imagined slicing open a pocket along the edge of her developing chest and inserting her butt fat there. Maybe then she'd be perfect enough for her Mama. She could make her freckles go away completely. Burn them off and smooth over the scar tissue with wax.

But on the inside, she knew there was nothing but blood and viscera. Muscle tissue and bone—insides that Mama would never see as anything but ugly.

Allison left Sara's veins alone and closed up her hand. The vessels ceased bulging with the lack of blood flow, but it didn't seem to matter now that her skin wasn't blushing and her heart stopped beating.

"I'm sorry." She glued Sara's mole back in place with a dab of hot wax. "You were perfect as you were."

For the first time in over a year, Allison disobeyed her Mama and went upstairs during the daytime. Scrawny legs carried her up the basement steps. She used her tools to pick the lock. Glaring white light smacked her in the face and she squinted to bring the world into focus. Wood-paneled walls held aluminum framed prints of flowers, but no photos of Allison. The memory of Allison had been wiped clean from the house long ago.

In the living room, pink boxes lined the shelves. Plastic dolls on display. Each one exactly the same. Grotesquely shaped pieces of plastic. Impossible standards for any person to live up to.

Mama slept in the reclining chair. Allison could escape, but she feared Mama would find her, make her keep fixing women who didn't need fixin'. Instead, Allison worked quickly wrapping duct tape around Mama's chest and the back of the chair. She secured her wrists to the armrests just as Mama opened her eyes.

"Allison! What are you doing?" She struggled in her binds.

"It smells bad in the basement."

"You can't be up here!"

"I shouldn't have to hide."

"Think about what you've done."

"I did what you asked me to do." Her voice trembled. "But it's never enough for you."

"What do you want? Wanna call the police? Show them what you did to all those ladies?"

"*I* didn't kill nobody!"

Mama shifted her shoulders but couldn't break free.

"Why did you have to kill them?"

Mama gritted her teeth. "They think they're so perfect. The pretty ones. They think they're sooooo beautiful." She smiled a maniacal grin, saliva stringing from lip to lip. "But they're not!"

Allison stood tall, wiping away tears. "Do you think I'm pretty, Mama?"

"Not when you act like this. Untie me now—"

Allison lifted her knife from the table and pointed it at her mother.

"What are you doing?"

Tears flooded her eyes and ran in a deluge down her cheeks. "Why is nobody ever good enough?" She pressed the tip of the knife against Mama's jugular notch.

Mama stiffened and whispered, "We can fix it. We can fix *you*."

"You can't change what I look like. I won't let you."

"Not what you look like. Your *habits*. Cutting things open. It ain't right. Something's not right with you. We can fix you...on the *inside*." Mama's eyes scanned her.

Maybe there was something wrong with Allison on the inside. Something not right. If she sliced open her own belly, plumes of pink ropes and gushing blood would spill to the floor. It'd be beautiful. But Mama would see otherwise. Mama's eyes ruin everything.

The stainless steel, three-inch blade pressed against her mother's cheek. "I think I know what the problem is, Mama."

"We can fix you," Mama repeated, trembling.

Allison set down the knife on the end table and tore a strip of duct tape from the roll. She pressed it to Mama's mouth. "I don't need to be fixed."

Allison grabbed the knife and gently jabbed it into Mama's eye socket, scraping bone at the edge of the brow. Mama's shrill gasp was muffled beneath tape.

She thrashed in the chair, but Allison was careful to work around her jerking movements. She swiped the blade in a circle. It snagged on muscle and connective tissue while making a loop—like scooping from a tub of ice cream. With the extraction of the knife, the eyeball plucked from the socket. It dangled there, a faucet of blood gushing around the tethered orb.

Mama passed out from the pain, and Allison went to work on the other eye. She cut each one free and dropped the crimson blade into Mama's lap.

"It's not them or me that needed fixin'," she whispered. "It's your *eyes*."

After removing the tape and laying Mama down, Allison bandaged the empty sockets and grabbed the loaf of white bread from the kitchen counter.

She opened the front door. Fresh spring air filled her lungs as she sat on the front step and pulled out a slice and took a bite. Nothing could hold Allison back now. Nothing could lock her in a basement, starve her, belittle her, and keep her down. She could do anything she wanted—become a doctor or a sculptor.

The world at her feet, possibilities endless, Allison, more than anything, wanted to be loved unconditionally. There had to be a family out there with open arms. A mama with eyes capable of seeing her beauty, every bloody bit of it.

RUTHIE'S GARDEN

Cassie Daley

NOW

Ruthie had been looking forward to tonight's dinner with her daughter for months. Jenna had three children of her own; her mother was happy for her, but often found herself missing Jenna's company. They had been close since Ruthie's husband passed, more like best friends as the two of them faced the world together.

Over the last few months, however, Ruthie could sense Jenna pulling away. In an effort to bridge the growing gap between them, Ruthie invited her to a family dinner. The time spent without seeing her daughter made her desperate; she was getting older, and she could feel every one of those years in her bones. She didn't want to spend the time she had left without her family.

Hurrying along with her food preparations, Ruthie glanced at the kitchen clock. Dinner was planned for seven, and she knew she'd have to rush if she wanted to finish everything in the remaining hour. Although her roasted chicken and freshly baked pies filled the kitchen with enticing aromas, Ruthie knew it was her side dishes of vegetables freshly harvested from her own garden that best displayed her culinary skills. Her pride and joy was a large group of tomato plants that produced the most delicious tomatoes anyone had ever tasted.

Ruthie suspected folks might take issue with the way

she went about growing such bountiful crops, but she didn't see the harm, not really. She even ate the vegetables herself, preferring the slight tang she found in them to the ones she'd tried from the store.

She'd take the secret of that flavor to her grave.

Ruthie started gardening when Jenna was a small girl. The cottage's location was perfect for the hobby, with a large, fertile backyard complete with an outdoor shed. The first year she planted her garden, Ruthie harvested veggies so ripe and uncharacteristically plentiful that she had to start giving them away to friends and neighbors, unable to eat all that she grew. She smiled each time she was complimented on the fruits of her labor, her outward grace and spoken thanks juxtaposed against memories tinged with blood.

The ding of the oven timer pulled Ruthie back to her dinner. She glanced again at the time; Jenna would be arriving soon. Eyeing the plates overflowing with steaming food, she nodded in satisfaction before hurrying off to clean herself up before dinner.

Forty minutes later, the doorbell to her cottage rang. The sounds of children's raucous laughter could be heard coming from behind the heavy front door, muted but happy. Ruthie rushed down the hall and onto the front porch, eager to see her daughter's face.

Jenna had grown into a beautiful woman, and Ruthie could admit that while also admitting her daughter didn't look a thing like her. She bore more resemblance to her golden-haired father, although Ruthie kept no photos in the house of her late husband.

Despite the setting sun, Jenna wore sunglasses on her heart-shaped face, shielding her eyes from view. She was tall and slender, a 'late bloomer' as the doctor said while she glared from the examination table at sixteen, concerned she still hadn't had her first period—or, more importantly to Jenna, that her chest was still as flat as it had been all her life. While the rest of her friends were shopping for revealing tops and flattering swimsuits, Jenna tried to hide away, ashamed of a body that didn't seem interested in growing with the rest of her. Although nature had eventually caught up, Jenna remained slight in frame, always looking a little bit vulnerable in her protective mother's eyes. Ruthie didn't think that feeling would ever go away, no matter how old her daughter got: she would always do whatever needed to be done to keep Jenna safe.

"I'm so sorry we're late, Momma," Jenna's voice held a forced lightness that Ruthie recognized immediately. "Steve had to work later than he expected, and Abby spilled milk on her dress in the car, so we had to turn around. I would've called, but my phone—"

Ruthie pulled Jenna into a fierce hug. "It's okay, sweetheart, I'm just glad you're here. And hello to *you* three!" Ruthie turned to her grandchildren, giving each a quick squeeze and a small tickle until they were giggling, staring up with bright eyed adoration for their doting grandmother. Her heart swelled, grateful to see her family again.

Behind Jenna, Ruthie spotted the man of the family lurking in the driveway. Ruthie had never been Steve's favorite person, and he certainly wasn't one of hers. He came from a wealthy family, and looked down on others less fortunate, a trait she didn't think Jenna had recognized in him until after they were married. She knew his presence in Jenna's life had a lot to do with the growing chasm between them.

"Good evening, Steve," she said. They made eye contact, and the anger in his eyes sent shivers down Ruthie's spine. The look he gave her was one she'd seen before, long ago, somewhere else, but never on him. She'd suspected before, but she hadn't been sure until now. She braced herself against the involuntary shudder she felt as she held his gaze. "Everything alright?"

He smiled, the anger disappearing as quickly as it came, a natural chameleon at home playing a part. He closed the gap between them, pulling Ruthie into a quick, uncomfortable hug.

"Of course! Sorry we're a little late, but we brought big appetites, didn't we?" The children vocalized their excited agreement, and Ruthie led the way inside, pushing the dark start of the night to the back of her mind.

Around the dinner table, Jenna's sons, twin seven-year-olds named Michael and Jensen, regaled her with tales of their preschool activities, excited to have their grandmother's undivided attention. Abby, younger than her brothers by four years, watched everyone with innocent curiosity, smiling occasionally when her brothers burst into laughter.

As the end of the evening approached, Ruthie found herself next to her daughter, washing and drying the dishes together as they had when she was a girl. She wrapped her arm around Jenna, squeezing. They made eye contact in their reflections mirrored in the window above the sink. Smiling at her mother, Jenna leaned her head over until it rested on Ruthie's shoulder.

"I'll try to bring the kids more. Steve works so much,

he likes to spend time at home when he isn't in the office." Ruthie forced a smile and hugged Jenna again, turning to kiss her gently on the top of her head the way she used to every night before bed. The excuses were no different than they had been for months, and she didn't want to end the night on a sour note by starting an argument.

Still holding her daughter close, Ruthie stared past their reflections to the yard outside, and the garden she'd worked so hard to keep alive over the years. A large rectangular plot of earth was freshly disturbed, the soil having been turned and tested earlier that afternoon in preparation for a replanting project that she'd had brewing for weeks now. It was a plan she hoped would bring her daughter back to her, safe from whatever dangers may be lurking.

"I know, baby. I'll see you and the kiddos again soon."

After her family had gone, Ruthie finished the rest of her clean-up and headed to her bedroom for the night. As she changed into her nightgown, she eyed the moon shining brightly in the bay window. The spot had been the thing to sell her on this cottage as a newlywed with her late husband, Alan. She'd envisioned herself on that ledge, surrounded by pillows and blankets, reading the mystery novels she loved so much.

Now, more than thirty years after seeing it for the first time, she sat down, her bones older and her body more stiff than they had been before. Gazing down into the dark backyard, she could just barely make out the tips of the trellises holding her prized tomato plants. She lost herself in the memories of the night she planted them.

THIRTY YEARS AGO

"Do you really have time for another hobby? The house needs cleaning, and dinner hasn't been ready until *after* I've gotten home every night this week." Alan stared at his wife as they stood in the gardening aisle, one of her hands clutching a packet of tomato seeds, the other wrapped around her swollen abdomen, eight months pregnant with her first child.

Ruthie's heart sank at his words, the response being both what she'd come to expect from him, yet still disappointing enough to elicit a physical response. She felt a tear slide down her cheek before she could hide it, and Alan's eyes narrowed in disgust.

"So you're gonna pull that shit again? Fine, throw them in there. It's always something with you, isn't it? You're never satisfied with what you have." He wheeled their shopping cart around on the last word, reaching over to pluck the seeds from Ruthie's hand, tossing them angrily in with the other items. She didn't even want them anymore but knew better than to say so. From her experience, resistance would lead to worse than a few mean words.

Ruthie knew the way Alan treated her was wrong, but she felt compelled to endure his abuse anyway. With each passing year, Alan's anger became harder for him to control, and all Ruthie could do was try to manage his moods before situations escalated.

She became adept at hiding her bruises, wearing sunglasses and long sleeves even on warm summer evenings. The few times she tried reaching out to her girlfriends, she had been met with uncomfortable stares and excuses on Alan's behalf. Behind her back, they gossiped in disbelief. Alan was one of the most popular men in their social circles, fortunate enough to have good looks and a fierce intellect. He was charming and manipulative, skilled at telling people what they wanted to hear—something Ruthie had realized much too late. Now she was trapped.

Shortly after giving birth to a perfect baby girl, Alan's behavior shifted. He became more gentle, and Ruthie hoped this would be the turning point they needed, the catalyst that would take their marriage from one of pain to something more tender. For months, he didn't raise a finger that wasn't in love, fulfilling the role of father figure better than Ruthie could have ever dreamed. She believed this was what she had spent so long suffering for: so this happy, loving life could be hers.

After months without incident, Ruthie forgot her own rules of placation. Her constant need to appease her husband for her own safety was outweighed by a sudden burst of anger as she witnessed Alan backhanding their daughter in her high chair for throwing a wet lump of food on Jenna's first birthday.

The heavy smack of his hand against soft flesh wasn't something Ruthie was unaccustomed to; she'd heard that again and again throughout their marriage, felt his anger connect with her physically in ways she wished she could forget. No, the slap wasn't what blinded her with rage, causing her to react. What she'd never heard follow that sound was the blood-curdling shriek her daughter let loose, devastated tears falling down her face as she stared up at her father in shock. He loomed over her, his fists balled at his sides, the mashed potatoes still dripping down the front of his work shirt.

Ruthie lunged at him, forcing herself between Alan and the high chair, her small hands pushing against his chest. She'd never fought back before, and recognized the danger of her position when she saw the hatred in Alan's eyes seconds before his fist connected with her face, spinning her around until she fell, her head smacking the wooden dining room table on her way down.

Her vision darkened and she struggled to clear her head, her thoughts fuzzy and hard to hold. The world seemed to dip in and out of focus, a ringing in her ears swallowing up the sounds of Alan's frantic apologies. She felt him kneeling beside her, and her vision swam as she tried to settle on his features above her.

"Ruthie, honey, I'm sorry. Please, I didn't mean to, I would never hurt you, you know that. I'm sorry, baby, are you okay? Can you hear me? Ruthie, say something to me." His voice rose an octave in panic, one hand reaching up to brush the hair from her face. As her vision cleared, she saw blood on his fingertips.

"I'm okay, it's okay," she began her familiar mantra, one she'd recited many times before. Ruthie's head spun as she remembered all the other times in a rush, the flood of violence and hurt and regret and shame she'd endured at Alan's hands washing over her like an angry red wave.

Lifting a hand, she felt the sticky, warm blood seeping from the cut on her forehead. Her head throbbed, the shock of the dual impact wearing off enough to finally bring the pain she knew was waiting. She faced her daughter, who sat watching her parents with fat tears still sliding down her cheeks.

"I'm going to grab some towels, and we'll get you

cleaned up. Don't move," Alan ordered before rushing off to the linen closet. She heard the door open and then slam shut, the anger in his voice already returning even as she sat on the dining room floor, bleeding. "Looks like someone forgot to do the laundry. I'll grab one from the bathroom."

As she listened to her husband rummaging around, Ruthie looked into her daughter's eyes and knew she had to act. Tonight's scene had shocked her; as many times as he laid hands on her, Ruthie never thought he'd ever raise a finger to Jenna. Alan hurting their daughter stunned her to her core. She'd always believed she'd been the reason for the abuse, that she'd done something wrong and if she could be a better wife, she could make Alan happy enough to stop lashing out in anger.

But Jenna? She was innocent, barely a year old and filled with nothing but light and love. She didn't deserve this. With an abrupt clarity she'd never felt before, Ruthie froze. *Neither* of them deserved this. There was nothing that could be done well enough or thoroughly enough to turn her husband into a better man, and it wasn't her responsibility to keep trying. She could see that now.

She heard Alan muttering to himself angrily from down the hall as she pulled herself up using the table, steadying herself with one hand. Her head swam with dizziness, but she knew she had to keep going. For herself, and for Jenna.

Leaning over their uneaten meal, Ruthie reached for the large carving knife jutting out from their pot roast. She wrapped her hand around the handle, feeling stronger than she had in years.

Ruthie didn't want her daughter to see what she was

about to do, even if she was too young to remember it later. Spinning around to face the hallway, Ruthie took three short steps in the direction of her husband, meeting him just inside the doorway on his return, safely out of Jenna's sight. Startled to see his wife upright and lurching at him, Alan froze, arms outstretched as if to catch Ruthie in an embrace.

She fell into his waiting arms knife-first, the sharp tip plunging deep into his stomach. The soft give of his plush midsection released a gush of hot blood on Ruthie's hand, and she struggled to keep her hold as her slippery hand lost its grip.

Alan used the last of his energy to fling his wife away as he sank to the floor. Blood soaked through the fabric of his shirt, the clump of mashed potatoes forgotten but still present, a reminder of what triggered the night's events. Even as he felt his life slipping away, he offered a bit of criticism to Ruthie, who watched with horror from where she'd been thrown. "The towels in the bathroom," he wheezed, struggling to catch his breath. "They're dirty."

Ruthie backed away from Alan's body, rushing to her daughter's side. She picked Jenna up and held her close, breathing in the scent of her baby soft hair. Mind racing, she felt the previous calm that had overtaken her begin to fade. What had she done? How was she going to raise her daughter alone?

Ruthie put Jenna to bed, careful to shield her from the mess in the hallway. Her little girl smiled at her from her crib, unaware of how different life would be for the two of them now. Ruthie smiled back, kissing her on the forehead, and then headed for the tarp in the garage.

If nobody believed her when Alan was alive, she had no reason to think that would change now that she'd killed him. She would say he'd been having an affair, that he'd disappeared with his lover. It wouldn't have been the first time he'd been caught cheating.

She felt the first whispers of guilt creeping in and shook her head. She wouldn't spend a single moment regretting doing what had to be done to protect her daughter, and herself.

Her eyes landed on the packet of tomato seeds from all those months ago. She remembered the harsh way Alan had spoken to her, and how later that night he'd apologized, only to leave bruises on her cheek a week later. She never worked up the courage to plant them, her goals of gardening lost under Alan's judging eye.

Closing her eyes briefly, Ruthie took a few calming breaths, steadying herself for what was to come. Visions of dirt clumps mixed with viscera flashed through her mind, the roots of new growth emerging from the edges of a ragged wound she'd inflicted. She pictured the face of the man she'd married, the father of her child, his mouth overrun with worms and other wriggling things seeking new life from death, their bodies creating pathways through deteriorating nasal passages and decaying brain matter.

Ruthie grabbed the packet of seeds, her shovel, the bundle of tarp, and got to work.

NOW

Ruthie crawled into bed, her arthritic bones creaking with each movement as she thought back to the earlier events of tonight's dinner. Replaying certain things that stood out to her in ways she knew her daughter didn't intend, like the way Jenna flinched when her husband leaned over to whisper in her ear as she reached for a second helping of mashed potatoes, a favorite staple from her childhood. Jenna put the spoon back down, her desire to eat forgotten with the message.

Ruthie thought back to the moments in the kitchen, the two of them washing up as they had so many times before. Even in the hazy reflection from the window, Ruthie could make out the soft bruising around Jenna's eye, not quite hidden beneath her make-up. She'd covered up enough of her own bruises to recognize the signs.

Before falling asleep, Ruthie thought of the phone call she'd give Steve the next morning inviting him back to the house to go over Jenna's upcoming birthday. She noticed recently that her tomatoes were looking smaller than usual, and if her plan went off without a hitch, she knew she'd get more than just Jenna back.

She'd been careful to measure her new garden plot to perfectly match her son-in-law's stocky frame. Smiling to herself, Ruthie drifted off to sleep, her thriving garden the last thing on her mind.

Her garden would grow, and so would they.

PLAYING WITH GODS AND DOLLS

Erin Al-Mehairi

Rebecca knew to keep to corners. Make friends with dust bunnies, cobwebs, and mice in the long-lost angles that no one ever had time to clean. At least in this large, colonial home there were spaces to slip into unseen. The air was so chilled from the hanging atmosphere of varying personalities that she preferred to linger behind the heavy, dark curtains.

She had to wear her hair in two very tight braids, and not only did they hurt her head from being pulled so taut by her mother, but they were the perfect thing to grab onto to inflict pain quickly and leave no marks. If she did something bad, her mother would scold her fiercely and slap her face. If she hid or went outside, and her older brother found her, he'd inflict much worse and laugh like it was a big joke. She knew sometimes when people are in pain they hide, and other times, they take out their anger on others. She was tired of both scenarios.

There was a bleak aura hanging over the beautiful estate, but the house was functioning enough with its ornate wallpaper and furniture, even if getting a bit worn. Her mother had switched all the window coverings to black and sent all the maids, cooks, farm, and home staff away once her father lost all their money on a bad real estate deal. Now he had to farm and fix and make do himself with the help of his children while his wife tended the house and kitchen. The once airy home filled with bright colors now had the heavy drapes drawn even during the day, casting a vignette hue. The atmosphere was stifling, with no sound of laughter or life. A surreal darkness swirled around the edges - one an oil lamp's flame could never dissipate. A damp that a fireplace could never quite warm.

Rebecca was a petite, thirteen-year-old with light brown hair and brown eyes, who loved to wear dresses and socks with lace on the cuffs. Her dress shoes were for Sunday best, but the rest of the time she wore ankle boots with flat soles, polished and protected from the elements by her father. That was because they were shoes you wore around the farmyard, tramped around the orchard in, and walked to school. One pair a year now, instead of two or three. She had to take care of them. She didn't want to go barefoot in the winter. That happened to one of her sisters. That, and a bunch of other unfortunate accidents that became instead, according to her parents, punishment for a string of bad behavior.

With her sister Leis disciplined in increasingly painful ways, Rebecca tried to disappear when she heard her screams. The smells of burning flesh made her stomach roll, and she shed a tear, which she swiftly wiped away, when she saw whip and branding marks on her sister's back as they changed for bed. She watched her sister's usually spunky demeanor change over time to one of silent sadness. Rebecca was sad for auburn-haired Leis, but also scared enough to keep quiet. Leis was fourteen, and so they were close, and she occasionally held Leis tight in the night helping to muffle her cries and subdue her nightmares. Eventually one morning last winter, Leis didn't come back to their room after punishment. Rebecca never saw or heard about Leis again. And of course, the rest of the children knew to not ask about anything they weren't told.

The rest of the family acted as if Leis had never existed. Ben was her older brother at seventeen, and her other older sister, Ruthie, was sixteen. Her younger brother, Simon, was eleven. Rebecca cried deeply inside, missing her closest sister. She would eventually turn her caretaking nature toward Simon.

Ben was able to do what he wanted, since he was the oldest son. If he'd had a good heart that would have been fine, but he had a wicked one. Ben would pull her hair in the yard when she was younger, and she'd cry out, but when their mother came, Ben would act like he was helping her. He'd tell their mother her hair got caught on the fence. Rebecca knew soon on to not point the finger at him. He was golden in her parent's minds and nothing would change that. Not even if he drew blood.

Boys and men like to test boundaries. That's what tall, strawberry blonde Ruthie would tell her, whispering into her ear when they were safely away from anyone's earshot. She told her he'd never quit, and for her to learn to avoid him or keep quiet about his harassment.

Ben only laughed at first when he pulled her braids, but now he sneered when he pulled her into deep barn corners, staring with dark black eyes when he took his knife and cut small marks under her breasts, at the very top of her thighs, in the crack behind her ear. She bit her lip to keep any noise inside and pulled spare fabric she'd snuck from the sewing room out of her dress pocket to wipe up the trickles and streams of blood. It excited him, inflicting pain on her. It wasn't ever long, for fear of being caught, but enough to make her feel ashamed and unworthy. Pain, inside and out. It also made her feel a deep-forming rage that seemed to bubble like lava just below the surface.

Afterward, he'd walk away from behind the shed or barn where he pulled her from view, and she watched him run his hand through his head of sandy blond hair and saunter away into the woods. Men and boys always loved to feel conquest, Ruthie had also said, no matter who or how. Ben was a master manipulator and her parents fed it and watched it grow while she festered in guilt. If her father found out, it would be her that would be beaten with the board of nails, not him. She stayed silent and hid in the alcoves and corners, telling only insects her secrets.

On the day her mother had a stroke, and died on the floor before her father could get in from where he was on the far end of the property (Simon and Rebecca crowded around her with no way to call for help, while Ruthie ran to find their father), she knew that life would only get worse. Their mother lashed out at the children, mostly abiding her husband in doling out punishments, but Rebecca had always had hope that a little bit of motherly nature would settle into her if she ever heard of Ben's abuse. Maybe it was a lie she told herself to keep going, but she'd never know now.

Their father became even more withdrawn and morose after their mother passed, often sitting hours a day by her grave on the hillside at the end of the tree line. He had dug her grave himself, even though her family from town had insisted on a proper burial by a grave digger and placement of a stone marker in the family plot. They wanted their priest to preside but instead they watched as her husband, sweaty and covered in dirt, held open his bible with his large hands and read. He put a wooden cross at the head of her grave and sat the rest of the night with her, everyone else long gone. They had headed out one by one, gossiping together about the plight of the children but not really doing anything either.

Rebecca grieved for her mother, or what her mother could have been, but more so for the hope now blackened. Ben became worse as his anger heightened, some related to his grief for his mother, who had spoiled him, and some related to the extra work his father was causing him either by being extra demanding or by just being derelict in his responsibilities all together because he was sitting at his mother's grave.

Ruthie often escaped to town and messed around with boys older than her. She wanted attention and a release from their dreadful life. She gave up on gentlemen and gave into pleasing men who didn't think she mattered. Perhaps she figured neither type of man thought she mattered. Rebecca knew if her father found out, Ruthie would be beat to a pulp. That was if he ever paid any notice. In the end her sister shacked up with a boy across town and her father didn't even seem to care. Her privileged life, expectations of a good match to a man with money and a reverence of Christ, were long gone when their father had lost all his money. Before, she'd always waste days away reading books and desired to further her education at a women's college. Now, her dreams forgotten, she'd probably end up pregnant and drunk given the demeanor of this gang of guys. Rebecca didn't even know which boy Ruthie had run off with, but she knew escape from their father and from Ben was her sister's real motive.

Now that both sisters were gone, this left Rebecca to do the one chore her father and Ben did seem to care about someone doing— cooking. She was stressed trying to learn how to cook and bake for her father and two brothers at only thirteen. Her mother never wanted her under foot in the kitchen and hadn't taught her a lick of anything necessary so she did the best she could with the ingredients she was given, which sometimes wasn't much.

One day she'd been making bread. Simon was helping her, but her father and Ben didn't like Simon in the kitchen even if he was still young. They wanted him to be a real man, they'd said. In order to make that so, Ben tied Simon to the kitchen chair with rope and made him watch as he heated a knife in the flames of the cook stove and then pulled up Rebecca's dress and placed it on her inner thigh. Her skin sizzled and melted creating the shape of the sharp utensil; the burning was intense, but she gripped the sink and dug deep within herself to steel against the pain. She had tried to fight him off as best she could, but he had gotten so strong from the farm work that when he gripped her, she couldn't really move. Screaming didn't help as her father was always so far removed from the house. Simon cried and Rebecca shouted at Ben to stop but he didn't care about what they wanted. He laughed maniacally and enjoyed her struggle, her pain, the smell of cooked flesh.

Held hostage in the chair, Simon squeezed his eyes shut and cried harder. Rebecca didn't scream or shut her eyes. She stared at Ben, shutting off her brain to anything but the anger building inside. Ben was in the throes of madness, pleasure, but the psychotic kind. She stilled and calmed herself, relaxing to try to make it hurt less. Without her fight, he quit. He was done anyway and turned his attention to Simon, telling him that's what a real man does, takes what he wants. After looking at him for a few moments, he left the house, leaving the screen door to slam behind him.

Rebecca understood then if he tired of her, he might start to torture and abuse her younger brother, too. Simon wasn't as strong-willed as the rest of them, and with difficulties at birth, he was small even for his age. Physically, he wouldn't be able to fight Ben off. She worried daily and tried to keep Simon with her so that Ben couldn't try to get pleasure out of hurting him physically. But if her father demanded Simon help him or Ben outside, and Simon was out there alone, there wasn't much she could do to protect him.

That night Rebecca rinsed her burns with cool, steeped tea and dried them, wrapping her legs in cotton strips. She laid awake thinking, staring into her dark ceiling, a small ray of light leaking in from the crack in the curtain. It was almost a full moon. Simon was sleeping in Ruthie's old bed, which was next to hers thankfully, so that only one fireplace needed to be used for heat. That was the excuse she gave her father, and maybe he thought his youngest child needed mothering, but she knew Simon simply was safer in the room with her. She could barely sleep anyway, but Ben seemed to slumber fine at night.

Rebecca fell asleep finally in the embrace of the moon's caress and woke up the next morning with a plan. She talked quietly with Simon before sending him down for bread with raspberry preserves for breakfast. Then, she put on her best dark pink dress which resembled the color of her favorite peonies, her white socks with the dainty edges, and her black dress shoes.

She watched out her upstairs window to see when Simon went outside. She had spoken to Simon about what she needed to do, and he had listened to her every word. He went out to find Ben and trick him into going inside one of the work barns. Once Simon turned the corner, she ran down the stairs and out, treading discreetly across the lawn and into the barn herself. She grabbed what she needed from the mounted wall hooks, a large metal hoe used in the garden, and molded herself into the shadows of an unused horse stall. She didn't feel nervous, just adrenaline, and so she waited.

Eventually she heard the voices of her brothers bickering as they entered the barn. As Simon was asking Ben to check on the feral animal he had spotted in the stall, Rebecca jumped from the shadows and brought a crushing blow down on Ben's head with the farm tool. Half of his head and face broke off, falling to the dirt floor like porcelain, shards and pieces strewn all over the ground. He looked like a stone doll, falling sideways with a rigid thud. There was no blood, no brain fluid or matter, easing out like a river. There was only emptiness and pieces.

Simon stared wide-eyed at Rebecca, less because she had murdered Ben, and more that their brother had cracked like a china plate. Ben's one dark eye left looked lifeless at them but she realized it was only a painted-on eye. Rebecca looked back at Simon in shock. She touched her own smooth skin, then Simon's cheek. Real. She bent down and touched the remaining part of Ben's face. Cold, hard. Why did he feel and look like porcelain?

She took her brother's hand and started running. She didn't even care about having on dress shoes, but led them into the forest, and they ran until they were spent. She'd expected her pink dress to be covered in blood. Now, she was clean except for dirt and leaves from the forest. She could walk anywhere, and no one would be suspicious, at least for now.

But the house kept calling to her to come home. Could she really go back? What would she do to claim back their lives? Was she lifeless, too? In that moment, she only felt free and empowered. She never wanted to feel otherwise again. The walls of that house were like a prison. She didn't want anyone to set boundaries for her life and she certainly didn't want hers tested ever again.

***

"Mom?"

Jen shook her head as a hand pulled on her shirt sleeve. It was her thirteen-year-old daughter, Marie. She looked at Marie, at her gentle brown eyes and silky light brown hair. Marie brought things into focus for her.

"Yes, honey?"

"Where were you? You seemed in a trance telling me that story," Marie said. "Then you stopped and were silent."

She handed her the next tiny piece of wallpaper for the wall in the bedroom of the old, colonial dollhouse they were renovating together.

"I was telling a story I think.... yes, I was, wasn't I? I'm sorry, that was quite a sad and graphic story for your age, but I didn't seem to have any control over telling it. It overcame me."

Jen looked down at the little doll in her hand, a young girl with a dark pink dress the color of peonies. She brushed the doll's hair softly with her fingers. She didn't want to lift the skirt to see if the doll had scars. That was a nonsensical thought she shook away.

"Well... yes... you were," Marie said. "But it's their story, I mean *her* story, isn't it? It's okay to tell Rebecca's story, Mom. Look."

Marie held up the teenage boy doll in a blue wool jacket for her mom to see. Half of his porcelain head was gone, a gaping hole where a portion of his face should be; shattered remnants nowhere to be found.

ROOM SEVEN

Gemma Amor

'We only have eight rooms,' she says, 'But they are each very well-appointed. Luxurious, but cosy. All the modern comforts.'

A hook board behind the woman holds eight keys. She gestures to them, smiling. 'You're the only guests in tonight, so take your pick. Although I can tell you that Room Two is our most popular. The bathroom, you see. A roll-top copper tub, perfect for a luxurious soak.'

I shake my head. 'My boyf...I mean, my husband asked me to find the quietest room possible.'

A fleeting frown scuds across the smile. She has caught my slip. Now, she knows why I am here. Her hand freezes on its trajectory towards the key for Room Two. I clear my throat, my face staining red, thinking, *Fuck*. No use playing it cool, not now. I must have expectation written all over me like graffiti. I am ripe with it, shoulders square, head back, shifting my weight from one foot to the other.

'Room Seven is perhaps the most...romantic,' she continues, smoothly, plucking a different key from the hook board.

'Room Seven sounds perfect,' I say, feeling like a child.

She waits for me to fill out my credit card details, exchanges them for the solid brass key, a key almost as big as my index finger. The heavy, cold weight of it is a surprise. It fills the palm of my hand, and I stare at it.

Am I really about to do this?

'Upstairs, and to the left,' the receptionist says, and I answer my own question, picking up my bag, letting my feet carry me to unchartered ground.

Her eyes watch me go.

***

An hour later, maybe two. It passes in a haze of anxiety. I drink to dull the edge of the blade in my guts. I look at myself in a full-length mirror as I wait. Am I thin enough? Do my tits still pass muster? Will the grey hairs be a problem? What of the silver stripes across the tops of my thighs, the creped skin around my belly button?

Am I reward enough?

A knock rings out.

He has come.

'Hi,' he says, and we embrace.

'Hi,' I say, and I can feel a prodigious heat gathering. 'Are we bad people?'

'Very bad.' He smiles, gently, to take the sting out of the words. 'There is no hope for us at all.'

His hands tremble, however, on my face.

***

'Tell me again about our house,' I gasp, and he laughs into my neck, fingers still working.

'Now?'

'Now...*Oh!*' I shudder into silence. He knows, instinctively, where to touch. I have spots, and he is claiming them, one by one. Digging for gold. Adventuring across my body, mapping new territory. Pioneers, both, or at least that's one way of looking at it.

Traitors, both, too.

'Well,' he says, then trails off, finding it hard to focus on more than one thing at a time. He has discovered a new locus and is engrossed. Playing me like a drum, my pulse staccato, I am a thunderous, thumping thing, and he moves in time with me. Over his shoulder, I open my eyes wide in surprise, coming into consciousness long enough to trace a crack in the ceiling of the hotel room above me. *Was that there before?* An idle thought, duly swept away by an explosion of warmth. I feel disassembled and rebuilt, reborn, remade, I feel…

The crystal chandelier fixed over the bed trembles.

'What was that?' I whisper. The room feels...different.

Smaller?

'Jesus, Lou, I'm close…' His breath hitches. He looks down at my face. Something in my brain short-circuits as his features crumble, his lower lip hangs loose, his eyes roll. This is a connection I have never known, never thought possible, until now. This is a piece of string, tied from his heart to mine, a ley line of recognition, a straight track from one country to another.

What am I going to do? I think, fighting back tears. *He is my One.*

Crystal droplets tremble again.

The crack in the ceiling widens, lengthens.

'Stop!' I cry, too late, from under the collapsed weight of him, for I see what is happening. The walls of Room Seven are shuddering, shaking, and moving inwards, towards where we lay upon the bed. Inch by inch, the ceiling moves downwards, and the vertices move sideways, and the space around us shrinks, grows fetid with our breath, the smell of our bodies, yet he cannot see it, he cannot see the fist as it closes, he cannot see anything right now, he is lost in his own heartbeat, a stressed, syncopated rhythm that pounds against my breast, disturbing the flow of the music we made.

I realise that the receptionist sent us to Room Seven for a reason. She has made a sacrifice of us, or an example.

Room Seven is hungry for sin, and the quivering walls are about to feed upon ours.

I thread my fingers through his thick, lustrous hair. A woman, reborn, only to be smothered, moments later, by circumstance.

Was it worth it?

I know in my heart that it was.

'I love you,' I say, and seconds later, the pain begins, and our flesh splits apart, ruptures like overripe fruit left stewing in the sun.

WATER BABIES

Sadie Hartmann

Katie sits on the edge of my bed and pouts. I see that same look on her face every time we get into a big argument. She wears her emotions. I keep mine hidden.

"What is it now, Katie?" I make sure to use my most exasperated tone of voice.

"I just want to go to the river one time with just the girls. No weed. No boys. Just us Water Babies. Why is it that we *never* do that?" She stretches her thin, tan legs and wiggles her freshly manicured toes. She uses air quotes for 'Water Babies.' A nickname our collective parents give us every time we escape to the river for the day.

I hate it when she uses air quotes.

I sit on the floor and bend one leg over the other so I can paint my own toenails. Katie's parents pay for everything. All her trips to the salon, clothes at the mall, they even paid for her bellybutton piercing on her birthday.

My vanity is self-funded.

Which is why I'm not.

Vain.

Like Katie.

"What if we compromise? Yes on the weed, but no boys?"

Katie sits silently for a minute.

"Fine," she says.

***

Hours later, after too many back-and-forth phone calls making plans and changing plans and re-making plans, we are finally on the road.

"I don't care if we listen to *Blood Sugar Sex Magik* again as long as you skip 'Under the Bridge.' They play that song on the radio every five minutes, and I'm sick of it." Katie digs around in her knapsack until she finds the CD and hands it to me. I'm pretty sure she's still butt hurt that I called shotgun again.

Our mutual friend Lilah is driving. She got a brand new car for her sixteenth birthday and is the only one in our friend group with a CD player in her car. She complains about driving us everywhere, but we try to make it worth her while with gas money or weed.

Katie and her friend Asha are in the back seat. This is only the second time I've hung around Asha and her presence makes me feel a little awkward; not myself. She's a hard read. A new girl at school. The rest of us have been going to the same schools since kindergarten. I slide the CD in and tap the button a few times until "Breaking the Girl" plays. My personal favorite.

"Good choice, Cat!" Asha says. I turn to smile at her, but her eyes are closed. She's mouthing the words to the song.

"She was a girl
Soft but estranged
We were the two
Our lives rearranged"

She rolls her window down and her long black hair swirls around her in a tornado.

The ride out to this fork of the Yuba River is a long one from my house. The highway eventually turns into a one-way dirt road that always freaks me out. You can't see cars coming from the opposite direction and people drive like assholes. I'm glad I'm not driving but being in the passenger seat is still nerve wracking.

"We're going upstream from Edward's Crossing right?" Asha asks.

"Oh, I don't think so," Lilah answers, bunching up her nose and looking in the rearview mirror at Asha. "We usually go downstream to the big swimming hole."

"Along with everyone else! I know of a more private swimming hole upstream if you guys don't mind rock-hopping for a while." Asha offers.

The car is quiet as we all contemplate this new development. I finally decide to agree with Asha as a gesture of breaking the ice between us.

"That sounds good actually. Especially if we're gonna smoke."

Nobody objects.

***

Rock-hopping is not my strong suit. The arches of my feet are extremely tender, and the rocks upstream gradually get more and more rough and jagged compared to the smooth boulders I'm used to. Katie offers to carry my knapsack for me as I struggle behind the other three girls who seem to fly over the rocks and are far ahead of me.

Finally, Asha yells back that I only have a little way

more to go. Looking ahead, I see that the girls are already laying out their towels for sunbathing and picking the best rocks. I curse under my breath, knowing I'll get some shitty rock to lie out on. I wish my friends were more loyal. It's hard to feel like I invest so much into my relationships when nobody does that for me.

When I arrive, I'm startled to see Katie passing around my pipe and weed.

"Jeeze, Katie. In a hurry much? I thought you didn't even want to smoke." I try to sound casual about it, like I don't really care, but I'm offended, and I hear it in my voice.

"Don't be so hostile! You still have to pick out your rock and stuff. We're just getting things ready."

I decide not to keep pressing, but I'm pretty bothered. It's hurtful that Katie didn't wait up for me or hold a good spot next to her so we could lie out next to each other. I hate that she seems more interested in Asha right now, even trying to perform for her with my weed. Smoking pot is my thing. Katie is acting like it's *her* thing.

I find a suitable rock and grab my pack from Katie. My towel barely stretches over the rough patches of the rock and when I sit on it, I feel pokey things snag my bathing suit.

"Dammit." I sound whinier than I want to.

"What?" Lilah asked.

"Nothing." I scan our surroundings and begin to feel better. The river snakes down between a canyon. Impossibly tall pine trees dot the sides of the ravine, but mostly it's the landscape near the riverbed I notice because it reminds me of what I imagine the moon looks like. All the granite boulders and rock outcroppings are shades of white or gray. Behind us, a thickly wooded area stretches for miles.

Nobody but us and an emerald green pool below to jump off our rocks into—it's beautiful.

"Ladies, I'm going to go check on that swimming hole upstream I told you about; make sure there are no naked hippies lying out." Asha giggles at her own joke.

I shield my eyes from the sun to look up at her. She's scratching at her chest, leaving angry, blotchy streaks.

"Asha, are you allergic to your sunscreen or something?"

She looks down at her chest, "Oh, um. Wow. Yeah, I guess."

"Hold on," I have too much shit in my knapsack, but I find what I'm looking for, "Here, aloe vera might help!"

Asha smiles as she takes the bottle and squirts some into her hand. "Thanks, Cat. I'll rub it in as I walk upstream." She hands me back the bottle, spins on her heel and disappears into the landscape of the rocks.

***

Lilah is a priss. I'm entertained watching her pack a bowl like she's going to get graded on it later. After taking a long hit, she passes it to me, her eyes darting around.

"So where did Asha go? We've been sitting here for like twenty minutes and she's still not back."

Katie stands up and pulls her bikini bottoms out of her crack and then looks long and hard upstream and downstream, shielding her eyes from the noon sun with her hand.

"Asha?" she calls out.

The rest of us pass around my pipe. On my second hit, I realize this is strong stuff and caution the girls against going back for too much. None of us are familiar with this swimming hole and it would be best not to be stoned out of our minds while we navigate it for the first time.

Exhaling a thick cloud of smoke, Lilah says, "So there's something I wanted to tell you in the car, but I didn't want to make things awkward. The reason none of the locals come here is that it's supposed to be haunted." Katie sits back down. Something about this one physical movement infuriates me.

"That's it? Your friend disappears and you call out to her one time and then just go back to smoking? Sorry, Lilah. I didn't mean to interrupt."

"What the fuck, Cat? You've been on my ass all day!"

I stare at Katie. She stares back. We challenge each other this way for a long minute.

"She told me her mom died out here a long time ago, ok? That's why she wanted to come to this spot. She's fine. She didn't want me to tell anyone but since you're kind of being a bitch, there ya go."

There's a collective stillness among us. The shock of her hostility and this news of Asha's mom's death is a lot.

"Okay, so that makes what I was going to tell you even more freaky. So like I was saying, this place is said to be haunted. A lady miner, back in the day, had a stake to this claim and she mined gold in the swimming hole upstream. She didn't know how to swim, and she drowned out here. Another group of miners eventually found her body and she had all these gold nuggets on her. They kept them and left her body to rot. She rage-haunts this exact spot apparently."

Katie snorts, "Good one, Lilah! You know, not everything in this town is haunted by fucking miners!"

"How do you know Asha can swim, Katie? Have you been to the river with her before? Not everyone is a Water Baby like us." I used air quotes. Mockingly.

"You know what? You're all a bunch of drama queens. Asha is fine. Give her some space. She's probably looking for her mom's memorial...thing. Thingie." Her hand gestures bother me.

"Or, maybe she slipped on a rock and hit her head and fell into the water too, Katie." I stand up. I know what it is I have to do. I have to be the friend to Asha that Katie isn't for any of us.

"Where are you going? She's fine!" Katie is yelling now.

"Maybe she is and maybe she's not. You can sit here and smoke all my weed, and I'll go make sure your friend's not dead." I grab up my towel and wrap it around my waist. I made a real effort to stomp off as well as I could considering the hot, craggy rocks still slow me down.

As I get further away, I can hear Katie's voice using pleading tones with Lilah. She can be so stubborn, so selfish. As I walk, I make plans in my mind of how I can start distancing myself from her. She's not a good friend. What if it were me? What if I had wandered off and was gone too long? She'd let me drown. She would.

The river is narrower up here and white with rapids. It's strange being next to a body of water I have spent every summer of my life swimming in but nothing about it seems familiar at the moment.

"Asha?" I yell with my hands cupped around my

mouth. My voice sounded so small compared to the roar of rushing water.

I finally get to a place where the rocks end and are met with the surrounding forest. The dirt and pine needles feel so much better on my raw, ravaged feet. Skirting close to the river's edge I find that there is another swimming hole up ahead. I spot a white cross with a wreath of flowers around it. I run up and search the water and surrounding beaches for Asha. Sparkle under the surface of the water catches my eye. Hobbling over the small, sharp pebbles of the beach, I finally get out into the deep pool.

Asha's eyes stare up at me from the bottom. She's deep. Way too deep. Her lips are parted. I don't see any bubbles escaping from her mouth or her nose.

My heart pounds in my chest. I'm too late.

I dive in, thrusting myself hard towards Asha. Swimming with my eyes open, I can see rays of sunlight striking through the murky green water, illuminating tiny motes of debris floating in front of my face. It's impossible to see anything more than a foot or so in front of me. And then I see Asha's face; her arm outstretched to me, her hand is limp and gently swaying with the movement of the water.

Oh god, please don't be dead. Please don't be dead.

I grab hold of Asha's hand and pull. Her body freely drifts toward me. I turn to swim up to the surface and pull her up with me when suddenly, she holds fast. I whip my head around and see another face below in the darkness by Asha's feet.

I find myself staring into eyes that look like white marbles pushed into a crumpled Halloween mask.

The mouth is curled in a snarl. When I open my mouth

to scream, big bubbles escape and I can't see. Panic and confusion trigger a flight or fight response.

Holding tight to Asha, I swim hard towards the surface, but she won't budge. A quick glance shows white fingers gripping Asha's ankle so hard, I can see deep divots where fingertips sink into her flesh.

Using my feet, I kick water at the creature in an attempt to get its grip to loosen. A loud screech sounds off in the water. I yank Asha's arm one more time. My chest is screaming for air, but I know if I give up or let go, I won't have another chance. Whatever is down here will hide Asha from ever being found again.

Surprisingly, her body crashes into mine and I push her up toward the surface. I swim up hard behind her, all the while thinking that at any moment, something will grab my ankle. My feet are kicking frantically and furiously in all directions hoping that speed and force will prevent anything from being able to get a hold of me. Finally, I break the surface and suck in air. Asha's body floats just a few feet away. I push her towards the beach. As soon as I can touch it, I stand and charge through the water, pulling Asha behind me.

I sink to my knees on the beach; it's hard to breathe. Air fills my lungs in ragged sobs.

Asha is lying face down beside me. Her skin is blue. It hurts to even look at her. I feel sick.

When I flip Asha over, I know she's gone. Her lips are a pale purple, her eyes stare past me.

Shuddering, my shaking fingers brush strands of Asha's slippery hair away from her face and chest. Maybe I can save her with CPR compressions.

The word "MINE" is scratched into her skin just

below her collarbones.

The letters are red and puffy, fresh. Scrambling away from Asha's defiled body, I crash into the small wooden cross. I look back at the swimming hole. A leering face is half in and half out of the water. Frozen with fear, hardly able to draw breath, I do nothing but look into those milky-white orbs staring at me. The head suddenly snaps back. A large gaping mouth opens wide with a throaty, guttural scream, "MINE!"

The sound is like an alarm jolting me from my paralysis. I scramble to my feet and sprint through the woods back to my friends.

I couldn't save Asha, but I can make it so that nobody ever comes here again.

WOMAN. MOTHER. GODDESS. DEATH.

Lilyn George

Before I died, I hated "girl comes back from the dead to seek revenge" stories. For one, they hardly ever explained the woo-woo to make it possible. For another, I just couldn't buy that those women mustered the strength to come back for revenge, you know? Once I died—crossed through that invisible veil of unrealized wishes and memories unmade—I realized there was only one force strong enough to allow someone to tear their way through that one-way gatekeeper. My baby needed me. Someone had hurt her in ways no one should ever hurt a little girl. Not just someone, but the man who had promised me that he would raise her like she was his blood. Now, I was going to kill that motherfucker in ways I couldn't have before I died.

See, I used to be afraid of going to whatever version of hell actually existed, but behind the veil I learned:

There is no Heaven.

There is no Hell.

Just the gray, the memories, and last night, the piercing screams of my baby girl as that son of a bitch took what was hers to give.

Even as I was scrambling back inside the disgusting, rotting body once mine, I knew there was no possible way my brain should work. The brain is one of the first things to break down in the body and even with a successful merge, I should have been unable to move, to think, to exist.

But I thought. I moved. I didn't exist—I fucking lived. At least as much as one can live in a body eaten by gut bacteria and other stuff I really didn't want to think about. I shoved my eyeballs back in their sockets and ripped ass in a fearsome and deadly fashion to rid myself of the gaseous bloat. My tongue was thick, and I couldn't get it to stay in my mouth no matter how hard I tried, so after a moment I gave up. I didn't need a working mouth to do what I planned on doing. However, to my delight, I discovered when I started clawing and punching at the coffin—desperate to free myself from the grave—I now had no working nerve endings.

Halle-fucking-lujah, all it took was coming back from the dead for the constant haze of pain to leave my mind. Who'd'a thunk it? Now I just had to get free. To find that bottom-feeding asshole that told me after those bullets had ripped through my body that he'd take care of my baby girl, and then done what he did.

By the time I'd broken through the cheap pine casket, my fingernails had broken off, along with the whole first section of finger on each hand. But that was okay. I could still bend my hand. Still had some mobility. I could do what needed to be done. I didn't need to breathe, so I let the dirt collapse on me, shoveled it to the side, packed it down. When I could sit up, I did. When I could stand, I stood still and reached out with the connection I barely understood to find my daughter. I couldn't delay. Though I'd ripped a hole in the veil, I wasn't free of it. It called me back so strongly that only my need to get revenge and protect my baby enabled me to keep going forward.

She was crying in her bedroom, chair against the door in case the asshole tried to come back in.

I'm coming, baby. This asshole won't get a chance to do you wrong ever again. To do anyone wrong ever again. I shoulda known something was fishy about that tallow-skinned, stringy-bean motherfucker. I shoulda—I stopped the self-doubt and guilt. It would only get in the way, and Mama had a job to do. I was gonna see my baby set right.

At first, I just wanted to run straight for her, but it takes a few minutes to coax atrophied, larva-infested muscles into moving. (Why the fuck hadn't I been embalmed? Even with a cheap ass casket, they shoulda done out with the blood, in with the chemicals and the ubiquitous anal plug not for anyone's using pleasure.) I looked at my blackened skin, the bloating, and realized there could be no real reunion with my baby girl. I'd scare the ever-lovin' bejesus out of her. After about five minutes of cursing and struggling with legs that wanted to fall back down, I finally got moving. Turns out walking, then running, are like riding a bike. Once I managed the first step, I was golden.

I was glad it was dark as I set off to cross the three miles of city streets that led to the home my little girl shared with that walking pedo shit-stain. I did not need to be captured on YouTube. I had a job to do. After I offed him, she'd have to go into foster care, but it was the best I could do.

I started off at a slow trot and somehow gained speed like the little engine who could. The thought that a woman can be many things simultaneously, and fiction is famous for being unable to take this into consideration, crossed my mind. But this isn't fiction.

I am Woman, and my vagina is infinitely tougher than a man's delicate little balls.

I am Mother, and the life I brought into this world is one I have a sacred duty to protect.

I am Goddess, temporarily freed from death, and a certain baby-fucker is going to hear me roar.

Those tenets, and the memory of my eleven-year-old's screams, pulled me through the streets with a swiftness I did not think possible. Her muffled sobs kept the tank of emotions driving me fully topped, gave me the power to lift my legs up one by one—using my hands to bend my knees when they suddenly refused to work—and make it to the third floor apartment where I lived with my daughter for nine of her eleven years by myself, and for two years with the man I thought would be a good father for my daughter.

I leaned on the door, hands grasping the handle, and tried to call out, but a low, garbled moan was all I could manage. I attempted to twist the knob, but the blackened skin of my palms sloughed off. It dangled toward the floor, held on by a thin strip of skin that—as I looked—disintegrated until the flesh made solid, sloppy contact with the thread-bare, puke green carpet.

Well, fuck. I eyed the meat of my palm, eyed the knob. I was sure for a split-second it started to turn. Was it possible the dumb ass didn't lock the door again? Scowling, I lifted my grime-caked, ugly skirt and wrapped my palm around it for traction. Worked for opening jars, right? Worked in this case too, though the effort I put in it dislocated my wrist. But, no nerve endings, no pain, so after the door clicked open, I twisted and fussed with the bone until a click told me it was at least back in place.

I took a breath which let me understand how a death rattle sounded, placed my palms against the door, and shoved it so hard when it slammed back against the wall, the knob crashed through the flimsy drywall.

Jason Sebastian Richards, in a sweat-stained undershirt that hung off his bony frame and boxers that looked like they could stand up on their own, jumped to his feet. He put a hand to his heart and his constant excuse of a 'bad heart' to get out of doing pretty much anything flashed through my mind. How had I not seen how pathetic he was while I was still alive? I slapped at the light switch as he scowled and said, "I don't know what you're playing at, but I wa—"

The light clicked on.

His eyes went pug-wide and the hand over his heart clenched into a fist.

I grabbed for the door, found the knob, and yanked it closed. It slammed shut behind me, but I didn't care because I knew no neighbors would come to investigate. Wasn't that type of neighborhood. Instantly, the stink of me became the prevalent smell, though the beer, sweat, and fear emanating from him was a close second.

My former fiancé said my name.

I snarled and lunged, felt my tongue drop out of my mouth as soon as I opened it. I ignored it, even when it squished underneath my left foot, much more concerned with getting to him. I'd rip his fucking tongue out so that he couldn't say my name or hers ever again.

His eyes rolled back in his head and the smell of urine added to the eau de death and slob stinking up the room. He collapsed in a heap right before I got to him.

It threw me off, I'll admit. I cocked my head, hauled back my foot and slammed it into his side. I heard a faint crunch I couldn't tell the origin of, but he didn't even moan. I did it again, harder. Still nothing. The reality of what had happened finally clicked. The sonofabitch had died of fright. Died before I'd even had a chance to… rage filled me. I stomped over to his corpse, fisted my hands in the pungent undershirt, and roared, "You come back! I'm not finished with you!" What came out of my mouth had been garbled and thick, and I spattered his face and chest with flecks of something foul and squirming.

I didn't expect it to work.

By all rights, it shouldn't have.

But my connection with death, with undeath, apparently had a trick up its sleeve. Within a second of my command, the fucknubblet's eyes popped open, and he drew in a desperate, lung-filling breath. A breath he tried to turn into a scream when he saw my maggot-ridden face so close to his, but I delivered a punch to his diaphragm, that had him turning purple instead.

While he gasped and cried, curled up on the beer-soaked recliner, I grabbed the duct-tape from its spot on the shelf, and with fumbling nubs of fingers, attempted to tear off a strip. When that failed, I attempted to peel a piece backward with my mouth. That small force cost me three teeth before I gave up. In desperation before I ran out of time, I shucked my skirt and underwear. I picked up the underwear and eyed the crusts of blood, shit, and some weird mucous I did not want to know the origin of that covered the formerly white material.

I balled them up in one hand and gave the baby-fucker a now very-gapped smile as I shoved his head back and thrust the material inside his mouth. It took about five seconds before he started to gag. I went to the third-hand stereo system, which had lived in our house longer than he had, and turned up the music enough to hopefully muffle anything Baby Girl might hear, though my connection to her told me she was still pretty oblivious to her surroundings. Then I picked up my skirt and tore it into three very long strips (so much easier than duct tape) and clumsily bound him to the chair. My third move retrieved an unwashed butter knife from the sink and a bottle of hot sauce from the fridge.

As I walked back in front of him, his eyes fell on the dull knife and the hot sauce, and he screamed in high-pitch terror until I temporarily buried the butter knife in his trachea. As he gasped for air, I reached in the slit of his boxers and pulled out the couple-inch long skinny worm he had been so proud of.

He proclaimed his innocence. It's amazing how, with a gag in their mouth, people can still manage to get the gist of what they're saying across. At that moment I wished my tongue did work so I could tell the bastard exactly what I knew. But my silence enabled me to hear the soft steps coming down the hallway. Jason and I both froze, albeit for very different reasons. I sprang up to at least try to turn the light off, bury the room in dark, but my daughter's sweet voice said, "It's okay, Mama."

I tentatively turned toward her, gave her a smile with my eyes since my mouth didn't cooperate, did my best to mumble a back of the throat "Hey, baby girl." I'm not sure how much she understood, but I had to try.

She gave me a wan smile, then turned her attention to the man who'd molested her. The man who should have taken care of her. Her eyes were old and cold as she watched him, and he stared back at her with visible shivers as sweat coursed down his face. She turned her attention to the implements in my hands, and her eyes lit up in understanding and pleasure. I inclined my head.

She considered me for a second, then pulled one of the ever-present hair-ties off her wrist. "I think if you wrap a hair-tie around it tight, it won't bleed so much. I heard that's how they used to castrate cows and stuff." I tried to take the hair-tie from her, but that was fine motor control I no longer possessed. "It's okay, Mama. I can do it."

I didn't want her to. I hadn't wanted her to see any of this. I understood she needed to regain some of her power, but she didn't need to touch him. I looked between the two of them and shook my head, then said "No" as best I could. She got the gist and relief bloomed in her eyes. I pointed at the hair-tie then held up my good hand with the thumb and forefinger about two inches apart. She slipped the black band around my fingers and I turned my attention back to my ex.

He whimpered and then that fucker actually had the gall to scream at her to help him. At least, I think that's what he was saying in between heaves. I punched him in the face with my bad hand, and as blood trickled from his nose, I looked back at my baby girl and then pointed toward her room.

"Yeah. I'll go now." There were tears that glistened in her eyes still, but now they were tears of relief. "I love you, Mama. Always and forever."

I remembered the basic sign for I Love You and signed it to her. She blew me a kiss but didn't look back as I knelt down to start my task. I had raised my baby right, and I was never prouder of her than I was then, as I coated the edge of the butter knife in hot sauce and then set to work.

He died, screaming, two more times.

Each time, I brought him back.

It wasn't until I'd shoved the remains of his genitalia so far back into his throat he could presumably only breathe through the slit my knife had made in his trachea that I considered my work mostly done.

Jason Sebastian Richards stared at me with eyes swollen almost shut from how much he'd cried. I pondered, for a brief moment, letting him live as the nutless wonder he now was. But, ultimately, he'd hurt my baby. Living another second on this earth was a gift he didn't deserve. So I used the knife to punch a hole into the area just below where his ribs met in the middle, and used that hole to worm my hand inside his abdomen.

It took a few moments of grabbing the wrong organs before I felt the fading beat of his heart in my hand. And, because sometimes clichés happen for a reason, I tore that fucker out and bit a chunk out of it while it still beat.

And then I leaned back against the wall near the door, and let gravity carry me into a slow slide to the floor.

The veil reclaimed me slowly. I had time to savor the look of what I had done. To make sure that fucker could never hurt my baby (or anyone else) again.

I died a second time with an obscene, open-mouthed smile on my face. My final thoughts of my baby seamlessly intertwining with giggle-worthy glee as I wondered what the fuck the cops were going to think when she called 911 in a few hours.

I am Woman.
I am Mother.
I am Goddess.
I am Death and I am waiting.

POKE, STIR, FLESH, BONE

Amanda McHugh

He said he'd planned the perfect date, led her down a
secluded trail in the heart of Thacher Mountain, thirty
miles of scenic views surrounded by dense forest and
rough terrain. His hand warm in hers as the narrow path
emptied into a clearing enclosed by thick pines. He'd set
up a magnificent spread on a checkered blanket, opened
an expensive bottle of cabernet, and poured two delicate
flutes to toast their future.

Jamie wishes she'd gotten the chance to taste the wine
before the growling had started. She's never seen a wine
that nice up close before, and she wonders if she ever will
again.

"This way," she whispers, pressing her back into the
rough bark of a tree.

She can't think about fancy wines right now. She
needs to keep moving. They've been running for ten
minutes, chased by the shadows in the trees, and Jamie
feels the gap closing between them.

Tolliver follows, leaning against a massive oak
opposite her, and together, they wait.

Winded.

Alert.

Jamie plucks a twig from her dark hair and tosses it
aside. Normally, she'd have it secured in a ponytail, but
as this was a special occasion, she'd opted for voluptuous
old Hollywood waves, pinned behind her ear with a pearl

comb that had been her mother's.

Plastic is for strumpets, pearls are for wives, Jamie's mother had said on her eighteenth birthday, sliding the teeth through Jamie's bangs in some archaic rite of passage. Her hands on Jamie's shoulders like weighted angels. *There. The men at State will be lining up at your dorm door. You'll get a ring.*

Any ring, she meant, because to Jamie's mother, any ring was better than no ring.

Yet ten years have passed and a wife, she is not. Jamie blushes at the memory now, at the flutter in her heart when she secretly hoped Tolliver was going to ask *the* question.

Oh, how wrong I was, she thinks, tasting the grit in her teeth.

"I hate the woods," Tolliver grunts, trying to catch his breath. He clutches his arm, sweater torn open where the creature had attacked, striking from the tree in a gray blur before she'd screamed at him to run.

Jamie glares at Tolliver. "We could've done this at your place. Why did you want to come here if you hate the woods so much?"

They've been seeing each other for a month, yet any mention of going to his house, a tasteful two-story on the outskirts of the city, always ends in a fight.

"Doesn't fucking matter anymore, does it?" he hisses, peeking out from behind the wide trunk before grimacing at the blood crusting on his sleeve. "Christ, I'm gonna need stitches. Fuck, this hurts. I need to get to a hospital. Did you find my phone?"

"No, you must've dropped it," she says.

"Damn. Any service?" he asks.

She unzips her cross-body bag and checks her own phone. "Nope."

"Son of a bitch," he says, pushing his thick hair off his brow. The gesture seems vain in comparison to the rest of his disheveled appearance. "I don't know where we are. Should've stayed on the fucking path."

"Didn't have much choice, did we, Toll?" Jamie asks, though it's more of a statement than a question.

"Maybe if you hadn't been freaking the fuck out," he says. "Did you see where it went? What was that thing?"

"I—"

Snap.

She freezes. "Did you hear that?" Jamie whispers.

Tolliver presses a finger to his lips and holds a hand up—as if she'd need two signals to be quiet. As if she weren't capable of following directions.

This is your fault, she wants to say, but Jamie closes her eyes and concentrates on her breathing instead.

From her right, a grumbling. Low, at first, a warning before the storm breaks. Have they caught up that fast?

Tolliver doesn't hear it. With his pointed ears and sharp features, she thought he'd resembled a wolf on their first date, but in this moment, he looks more like a lamb awaiting the slaughter.

Not exactly the shining example of masculinity her mother had urged her to find. *A real man will be gentle yet tough, caring yet aloof. You'll require no explanation for either behavior because, above all, he will protect you.*

Most days, Jamie's glad her mother's not around to dole out any more warped pearls of wisdom. Since her death—a tragic accident, all the doctors agreed—Jamie's learned a lot about relationships, and any man worth her time, she realizes, will respect her ability to protect herself.

Crack.

The growl deepens.

"Tolliver," she whispers, squeezing his elbow. "It's here."

He shakes his head in disbelief. "I think we're okay."

The growl rips the air open.

Tolliver screams. "Fuck this, I'm not dying here."

Jamie reaches for him, but she feels his fingers digging into her chest, launching her backward. She trips over a root—because she's clumsier than a dancing bear, according to her deceased mother, not at all because Tolliver knocked her off-balance and fled like a coward—and falls hard on her tailbone. Jamie yelps at the sudden burst of pain radiating up her spine.

Tolliver doesn't look back. He disappears into the tree line, his footfalls thudding loudly in his haste to escape.

They say adversity brings out a person's true colors. Jamie, however, hates that expression. Colors can't be hidden, but people can blind themselves to what they don't want to see. Choice is a powerful thing.

Crack.

The growl is close but moving away from her.

Jamie finds her feet and brushes debris from her jeans. "Tolliver," she shouts, making herself bigger than she feels. Hurrying after him, she scans the knotted trunks for his shape.

"Tolliver!"

Crunch, crunch, crunch.

He hasn't made it far, she sees. Someone should've

told him to stay on the trail.

Zigzagging aimlessly, Tolliver gains another yard before a figure darts in front of him.

Fast, she thinks.

And long. Gray, the color of ash and charcoal. It moves lithely with the confidence of a predator who's done this before, a hundred times, a million, and in its measured steps, Jamie sees finality. Whatever Tolliver is thinking—if he even is thinking at this point, but she suspects he's running on adrenaline and cowardice—his plan is no match for the hunter's experience.

"Tolliver!"

He hesitates, but doesn't turn, looping his leg over the girth of a massive log. A mistake, she could've told him, if he'd bothered to listen for two goddamn seconds. The gray creature stalks closer. Jamie sees tufts of fur, two pert, triangular ears, a snout, and a mouth full of teeth.

Two icy eyes, eerie and omniscient, meet her gaze. It nods.

"Fucking fuck," she says.

She'd seen that look before. The Hunger. When she was thirteen and walking home from school. Her mother insisted she walk the two miles every day lest she succumb to the gluttonous tendencies she'd inherited from her father. *No man wants back fat*, she'd say, pinching the delicate flesh of Jamie's underarm.

On that particular afternoon, she'd cut through a random backyard to avoid creepy Mr. Hebstrom. The way he ogled her from the confines of his front porch, tongue flicking the corner of his mouth when she adjusted the hem of her skirt, it made her skin crawl.

She hopped the chain link fence. The dogs came out

of nowhere.

Four Siberian huskies. Hypnotizing in their identical stances, poised at intervals like majestic statues.

But they were also snarling, fangs bared beneath their wrinkled noses. Synchronized, they surrounded her, one nipping at her calf to distract her while the others took position, forming a circle with her at the center.

"Go on," she whimpered. "Get!"

One snapped. Then another. They growled and pawed at the ground.

She couldn't run without getting mauled, she knew that in her bones, so she roared and unhitched her book bag. *If I'm going to die*, she'd thought, *I'm going to do it fighting.*

Jamie swung with all her might. It connected above the shoulder blade of the first dog. She'd never been so grateful for homework. Lugging fifty pounds of textbooks had finally served a purpose. Another lunged. She felt the hard lines of his claws tearing through her sweatshirt as her bag connected with the third dog's snout.

The fourth latched onto her hip, trying to tug her to the ground.

A sharp whistle saved her, a woman with blood-red nails and a black velour tracksuit. She stood on the concrete steps at the back of the house watching the scene unfold. Her wild hair puffed in a corona around her head like she was engulfed in flames, but her eyes were made of ice, so blue they were almost white. Locked on Jamie.

"I'm sorry," Jamie said through gasps. "I was just trying to get home." She glanced toward Mr. Hebstrom's house, saw him pawing at the pleat of his pants as two girls strolled by.

Something passed over the woman's face. Recognition. Understanding. She smirked and nodded at the gate. "Brave girl," she said. "Don't apologize. We have to stick together."

In that moment, Jamie wanted to hug her, but she didn't, afraid the random show of affection would dull whatever kindness the woman was extending.

It wasn't until later that she realized that goodness of the woman's heart had nothing to do with letting her go. Young girls never realize that, one day, they'll be the women watching from the stoops.

And sometimes the kindness comes too late.

Tolliver's jeans snag on the bark.

Another growl sounds behind her, and Jamie quickens her pace.

The gray figure strikes, lightning across his body. Tolliver shrieks, reaches for his leg, and careens off the log.

"Get up," she commands, just a few yards from where he lies squirming on the ground.

"I can't." He lets the sentence draw out. *Caaaan't.* Like a bleat.

There's no sign of the one who attacked, but she feels their eyes nonetheless. "We need to keep moving," she says.

Tolliver groans. "My knee. The son of a bitch got my knee. Fuck, I can't walk."

"Poor baby." She crouches next to him to examine the damage.

He groans. "Help me. Hurry, before it comes back. We have to get out of here."

"We?" she says. "Don't you mean you?"

Tolliver sputters. He tries to sit up and howls at the pain, a fresh spurt of blood seeping from the wound. "I—I'm sorry. I freaked out, alright? I wasn't gonna leave you. That was—I thought you were right behind me."

The lies.

"Then maybe you shouldn't have pushed me," she says slowly.

"Fuck, Jamie, we can't do this right now." He scans the trees manically. "Look, I scared it off, but that thing could come back and tear you to shreds any minute. We have to get out of here. Be pissed all you want in the car but get me the fuck up!"

She waits a beat then gives him a sheepish smile. "Of course. Yeah, what am I doing?" She taps her forehead, *doh!*, and feigns rolling her eyes at her own silliness. "Vanessa would kill you if you didn't come home. Or she would have, if she weren't dead, but still, it's the principle of the matter. Can you hold your weight?"

The color drains from his face. "What did you say?"

"Can. You. Hold. Your. Weight?" Each word a punch.

"How do you know about Vanessa?" he asks.

Jamie's smile doesn't falter. She pulls the pearl comb from her hair and rubs it between her palms. "A magician never reveals her secrets."

Tolliver rolls, preparing to stand on his own. "You don't know shit."

Jamie watches him struggle. *Oblivious*, she thinks.

"I know you murdered your wife. In these woods, actually. Where you set up that romantic picnic. For us." She grins at his dawning horror. "Did you get some sort of sick pleasure out of it? Bringing me to the place where your wife took her last breath?"

"I don't know who put you up to this," he spits, "but I won't waste time with lawyers. Extortion, revenge, you're a fucking psycho—I don't give a fuck what your reason is, but I will find out who hired you, and when I do, you'll wish for death. I'll take everything you have and when you're writhing at my feet, begging for salvation, I will fucking bury you."

"Like you buried Vanessa? Or does that not count because you cut her up first." She taps the comb against her chin. "Think I'll take my chances."

"You don't want to do that, sweetheart. Believe me. I'm a man of my word."

"And I'm a woman of action." Jamie taps her ear. "Beta. You're a go."

Tolliver laughs. "What's that, the magic word? Abra cadabra. Open sesame! Watch The Great Jam-bini pull a rabbit from her hat." He stumbles, punch-drunk but amused.

Five figures emerge from the woods. They are wolves, but more.

Tolliver swivels at the sound of their arrival, limping in place without a clear exit. "Holy shit. Jamie, what is this?"

From her bag, Jamie takes the head and slides it over her own. Calling it a mask would be a disservice. Masks are for pretend.

This is an extension of my body, she thinks. *A second skin.*

"You want a magic word, Tolliver? I'll give you a word." Jamie passes the clip from one hand to the other. A few tweaks were all it had taken to alter its purpose, each prong equipped with a micro-dose of what she needed: restraint, paralysis, death.

"What the fuck are you talking about? Cut the bullshit and—"

Jamie sinks the teeth into the meat of his thigh. "Run."

Tolliver curses as the shot of epinephrine courses through his system. His blood vessels are narrowing. His airways are opening, and that'll feel *good*. He'll relish the energy. Believe he's invincible.

He runs.

And that's exactly what they want. Nothing falls harder than a false hero.

The wolves don't speak. They don't need to. Synchronized, they split into formation in pursuit of their prey.

Jamie is less steadfast without her gear, but terrain boots and an all-gray ensemble would've set off his alarm bells. Bait is vulnerable. Bait is subservient. Bait is pretty, much like her mother always wanted her to be before Jamie showed her the pack; what real love actually looks like.

She leaps, slides, and jumps without hesitation, breathing in the familiarity of the woods. Their territory. Their hunting grounds.

Tolliver, however, is proving to be a disappointment. Even with the epi injection, he's already slowed to a walk, propping himself up on trees and furtively looking over his shoulder.

Beta must've cut him too deep, Jamie thinks. *She'll have to be more vigilant next time.*

She finds the pearl comb lying in a tangle of weeds,

stained red but intact, and slips it into her bag.

Tau, Delta, Zeta, and Omega cut off his exits from their respective corners, slowly closing ground between them. They each hold a curved blade, five inches long, iridescent stainless steel sharpened to perfection.

"What do you want?" he shouts at them.

"*Whattayewwaaawnt*," Tau teases. Her voice is gruffer through the wolf head, but the British accent is unmistakable. "Gosh, how Vanessa managed to deal with your whining for as long as she did is a proper mystery."

"What do you *want*?" He repeats.

"Money," Beta says, stomping in from the rear with her own claw primed, and they explode in laughter.

"Fine, fine, how much?" he asks with nasally desperation.

"She's fucking with you. We don't want your money." Jamie secures her own blade, chosen in honor of the night, an inch longer than the others and pure Damascus. "We want to pick your bones clean."

Tolliver cries. "Why?"

Beta takes a step closer. Her wolf head is pristine, no matted fur or splatter stains, teeth as white as death and twice as lethal. "Vanessa was one of us. Our Alpha." She howls and the others join, a mournful, longing sound.

"You took her," Tau says, claiming another inch.

"You butchered her," Omega adds, matching her stride, voice thick with emotion.

"And then you tried to replace her." Jamie removes her head. Against their rules, but for him, she's willing to accept the consequences. "I thought you were the one, Tolliver, I really did."

"Jamie." He grunts. "Let me go." Sweat beads on his

forehead.

"We never use real names, so I didn't know you were Alpha's husband," Jamie says. "I knew she had a husband, of course, but we try not to bring our personal lives into the hunt. For obvious reasons, you understand. But one night Alpha didn't show." She levels with him. "Alpha never missed a hunt. Not a precedent you want to set as a leader, you know?"

"Vanessa wasn't a leader," he says.

"She made herself weak around you." Beta growls and lunges, but Delta holds her back.

"We went to your house," Jamie says. "It's beautiful, you know. I could never understand why you didn't want to take me home. I thought it had to be me. Until that night. When we saw you load the shovel into your car. And followed you to the woods. And I realized Alpha's husband and my boyfriend…were the same person."

"Vanessa deserved better."

The others sound agreement. Their howls fill the trees.

Tolliver grabs for Jamie. "You were the one I wanted. Vanessa was…was an accident, I swear. You can't listen to them, they're lying. Jealous."

"Funny thing about women who find their pack," Jamie says. "We adapt. We survive." She grabs the sides of his head and kisses him. His breath is rank, but she makes it count.

"This could work, me and you," he says when their lips part. "Give us a chance."

"Oh, baby," she croons. "You're out of chances."

She hasn't released her grip. Perhaps he sees the intention in her eyes. *One of the many reasons we keep our heads on,* Jamie thinks. *Prey can always sense the truth.*

Before he can slip out of her grasp, she bares her teeth and clamps down on his nose. Through skin and gristle. Metallic tang explodes in her mouth. She gags but holds tight.

He screams and punches at her, pulls her hair and digs his nails into her cheeks. She's bleeding, but the rush is exquisite—pain, thrill, all of it, exhilarating.

Beta roars and makes the first slice, severing Tolliver's Achilles.

He won't be running anymore, Jamie thinks, as she spits out his nose into the forest. She wonders which woodland creature will reap the benefits. A squirrel, maybe. Or a fox.

Tolliver collapses, staring cross-eyed at the hole where his nose used to be.

Tau is next. Her claw separates his hairline from his skull. The flow is immediate, the stench of the kill in the air. Intoxicating. Driving their hunger.

Zeta and Omega strike on either side, disabling his flailing arms with their steel.

Lowering herself onto his trembling torso, blood running into his eyes, his moans are constant. Jamie readies her claw in a reverse grip. There is no goodbye, no final word or witty Final Girl catchphrase.

There is only her blade as his neck unzippers.

Jamie replaces her head. The wolves link arms. They watch.

In silence, they break him down as he'd done to one of their own and would never do again.

They peel his flesh. Pick his bones. The rest, they

leave behind.

A MARRIAGE OF DUST AND BLOOD

Michelle Garza and Melissa Lason

The girl spins. She holds her arms out, feeling the breeze sweep through her hair. A veil made of a thin scarf falls from her head as she gathers speed. She tilts her head back and smiles as she tosses a bouquet of haggard wildflowers to an imaginary crowd. She is a bride, but she is morphing, the imagination of a child changes quickly. Her tiny bones are shifting as the world spins with her. She pictures herself as a delicate bird with wings sprouting soft feathers. The sun circling overhead is like a blinding eye watching her. She can't bear to look at it, so she closes her eyes. A shouting breaks through the haze of her daydream. She stumbles as she turns. She is a bird, a little sparrow, spiraling from the heavens, caught in a dizzying nosedive. The sky is rejecting her to her doom. The grass awaits her landing, but so do the stones hidden in it. Her knees are sliced wide open in an instant of searing pain. Her blood runs warm down her legs as she stands, her head still spinning. She has torn holes in her dress and her flesh. Her mother won't be happy at all, and her father, he'd be unrelenting. A booming voice echoes from the house, it sends a shock through her. A giant is hollering, shattering her happiness. He shouts words at her mother, things men shouldn't say to women. It reminds her she doesn't live in her fantasy world; no gentlemanly prince was coming to marry her and take her away. She is not a sparrow riding the breeze. She is not a bird, or a bride. She is a little girl, not strong enough to fight. She is a little girl, doomed to the fate she was born to.

***

"You expect *me* to marry *you*?" his voice is barely a whisper above the wind, but she knows it will grow until it is the only thing she can hear.

"You promised you'd make a good wife, better than what you were before…"

He uses her past like a weapon against her. He threatens to take away the future he promised her, a wedding and an honest life out West. She can't say why those things became so important to her, probably because he ground them into her mind until his wants took over her own. She is a somnambulist programmed to sleepwalk to the beating of his drumming voice, and to ache solely for the dreams he proclaims only he can offer her. His reputation is his shield, his notoriety a sword which could cut her in two if she told anyone of the real man hiding beneath his pious façade. She remains silent while the outside world adores him, her heart knows the truth.

John's eyes still rove over her on occasion, hesitating lustfully on her breasts. It's when his face grows sour that she knows his God has poisoned him more than any liquor he once consumed. She can see the accusations in his eyes, how she led him astray, even though he was already on his way to the fictional Hell he feared so much long before she gave into his sexual advances. She satisfied both their longings, and in return he made her feel ashamed for not denying him. She often wondered if he didn't propose out of some guilt he felt for the nights they spent more akin to pagan deities, naked and sweat-drenched, their mouths tasting of wine and desire. Was he marrying her to satisfy God? Did he only want to mold her into a bible-toting woman of piety, did he take her so far from home to hide the fact that he too once reveled in sin?

Her feelings for him are ugly things hidden beneath the rib cage, love and hate stitched together in a scar tissue puzzle. They hurt, wept, and bled together. The truth festered there until the pain was unrelenting and shame blossomed out of control like black fungus from keeping secrets hidden in that darkness where no light or justice ever shines.

Aida's body trembles as she hands him a cup. She restrained herself from holding the boiling pot too close to him, it would be far too tempting not to empty it over his head and scald his mouth shut for good. She lets it rest in the sandy earth, and doesn't even think of filling her own mug, not until he tells her to.

The dark, rough material of her dress does nothing against the encroaching darkness, a savage desolation she had never experienced. Her skin is cold, too cold even for a winter night. It felt like the desert was swallowing them. It took all of her strength to hold herself together. She didn't want to disappoint him or to make him angry at her. This was going to be a new beginning for her, for them. She didn't want to ruin it by having him remind her of the power he held over her, how she was nothing without him. The wind blew and cut right through her, but he offered her no warmth, of body or soul. She was not built for such a trip, but she didn't voice her fear, his eyes were on her.

He spits his coffee out without swallowing the hesitant sip he brought into his mouth.

"Piss poor!"

He empties the cup into the dirt and turns to her, his eyes are angry, as they always seem to be lately. They were not the eyes of the man who wooed her; those had been hidden for years. They accuse her of purposefully spoiling his coffee, "Are you tryin' to kill me with this garbage?"

She backs away, shrinking as small as she possibly can, averting her eyes, and shaking her head. She is a startled mouse, and he is the giant towering over her with a heavy boot constantly lifted above her. She dares not speak too loudly. She dares not to make him feel challenged.

"No, John."

"I know you are an orphan, but didn't anyone teach you anything about being a woman?"

She is silent but her eyes meet his for a moment, she knows he can read her thoughts in that instant. She knows it's a mistake. She lowers her eyes again.

"You did that on purpose, right? Still tryin' to get back at me for not payin' for a stage coach?"

"No."

"You think I'm cheap. You didn't say it, but I can see it clear as day in your face."

"I wouldn't dare. I know you were just tryin' to save a little for when we get there, honey." she smiles but it holds no joy, only a plea for him to calm down.

He scoffs, his shadow is blocking the comforting light and warmth of the fire. "When did you become so sweet?"

"I know you're doin' your best."

"Now you agree with me, when for three days you've looked at me with that sour face, accusin' me of gettin' us lost out here."

Aida stays silent. She knows where an argument would lead.

"What would you know? You can't even make a proper cup of coffee."

She shies away and picks up the coffee pot with a tick towel to guard her palms, not speaking another word. Aida can feel his anger radiating off of him, hotter and more volatile than their fire. He is ready to take out all of his frustrations over his failures on her.

"Get rid of that garbage!"

She carries the coffee pot into the dark and pours it into the sand, her attempt at making him happy goes steaming into dry brush. She was cold, and even if the coffee was bad, she still would have wanted a cup, but she wouldn't dare make John think she was questioning him. He was a horrible man now most of the time, but she had no one else.

The desert around her is watching, waiting. The cold snaps at her like a hungry dog, biting into her cheeks. Winter in the desert surprised her. It was a different kind of cold she had never experienced, such a desolate chill, but she preferred it to her fiancé's company now that he had the mind to fight with her.

She comes to a stop beside of the horses. They fidget and turn to her with large eyes, full of knowing and solidarity for they too were abused by John. They were all only tools to him, things to accomplish what he wanted and only what he wanted. If they failed to obey him, he would cuss and kick them. She runs her fingers through their manes. She shares their anguish and concern. She silently promises to spoil them if they only carry her to some civilized place beyond all the cactus and snakes.

He sits staring into the fire, his cheeks burning but not from its heat. For a moment he let his mind wander, he thought of how it would feel to release all of his frustrations in a night of passion with Aida. His hands trembling at the thoughts of stripping the dark dress from her body, how many times he had denied himself and her. His anger rose to devour the sinful images, he is left ashamed of himself and how he once lived. His eyes glare into the night, to where Aida had been. He blames her. His hand scrambles to a pack at his feet, his bible is waiting. He opens it and lets his finger fall, and his eyes grow wide at the verse beneath it, as if God wanted to remind him of the new path he chose for himself…and for Aida.

"What comes out of a person is what defiles him. For from within, out of our heart of man, come evil thoughts, sexual immorality, theft, murder, adultery, coveting, wickedness, deceit, sensuality, envy, slander, pride, foolishness. All these evil things come from within, and they defile a person."

His voice breaks through the growing wind. Reciting bible verses, as he did most nights now after giving up the liquor. She resents it, his nightly routine, and marvels at how much he has changed. She longs for the time when he held a bottle in his hand, at least then most nights he'd pretend to love her. He'd whisper sweet words in her ear as he ran his hands up her skirt. His tongue was good for something once upon a time, but now he wouldn't even do that. That was before his father, on his deathbed, condemned his son for living in sin, with his whore and his liquor. It dug a hole in John, one he tried to fill with the bible. Daily he tried to appease a dead man and not himself. He was afraid of sin, and that's all Aida was to him, a shameful thing he helped create.

She was once a dancer, an artist, an untamed soul. She once felt like she could soar higher than heaven until he came along and trapped her, captured and caged her like a bird. His words, his expectations, his demands, they had built a prison around her with his promises of marriage until she was nothing but a ghost of herself. She felt it like a knife driven slowly into her heart, the realization of lost potential, of her dreams languishing on their deathbeds while she aged prematurely and watched them slipping away. He once swore he was enamored by her spirit, but now he only wanted to stifle it, to stomp it out like glowing embers into the dust until it was dead. He didn't want to marry her, he wanted to own her. It was a horrifying realization she couldn't escape.

"What makes you think *I'd* marry *you*?" she poses the question to the darkness, mocking him, wishing she would have thrown the coffee in his face. Her *old self* certainly would have.

"Refuse'im." A whispering voice makes her heart stutter, it's hardly audible and scratchy.

She spins slowly and sees the twisted silhouette of a tree against a storm-laden sky. Its branches are dotted with the forms of large birds. She wonders for a moment in her exhaustion if it isn't all in her imagination.

"His empty promises keep you chained to'im."

"Who're you?" she asks, squinting, eyes searching and finding no human.

Her arms tingle, each delicate hair standing up on end. She trembles but stands as still as stone as the atmosphere grows statically charged, like lightning was ready to strike her. She feels it dangerously running over her and through her, opening something within her mind and soul.

"A man should be your equal, not your master, little sparrow."

The words stung. The truth in them was like a vivisection performed by unseen hands, opening her up. She shuffles backwards. Her trembling hand abandons the coffee pot she still carried. It lands in the sand as a cold wind sweeps over her face. Lightning plays across the distant horizon, glowing brighter, a storm was building and now it is bearing down on her. The tree is filled with vultures, their bald heads titled to the side. The sight of them sends a shock through her, her mind thinks only of death. The voice becomes clearer, and so does her recollection. It was one she knew.

"Leave'im out here with the other snakes and scorpions."

The voice ate its way into her mind, a vault of memories she fought to keep sealed. Painful recognition struck her, "Mother?"

"Don't tell me you forgot about me."

She wrings her hands but doesn't say a word. How could she forget?

She would never forget.

"I always hoped my little sparrow would fly so high, but instead, you became me."

The nickname her mother always used for her broke her heart.

"Why're you still out here in the dark?" His voice nearly stops her heart, it is as hard as stone and as sharp as the spines of the cactus hiding amidst the Creosote.

Aida doesn't answer. She doesn't dare speak of her mother. She never told anyone, especially not John.

"Get back to camp." He says and turns his back to her, not offering her his hand in the dark.

She quickly retrieves the coffee pot and follows along behind him like an obedient dog, a packhorse laden with his belongings. She feels her mother's eyes on her, and in the howling winds the smell of rain comes, but it's not heavy with the scent of wet Creosote like the nights before but with ash and a note of copper. She no longer felt the desert was so desolate and lonesome, out among the quaking palo verde and rustling brush was her past. It was perched in a tree among the vultures, waiting for death. She hoped it wouldn't be her own.

The night was an uncomfortable dance of trying to keep warm and dry all the while avoiding his gaze. He refused to lie down next to her or shelter her when the rain came down in a quick sheet before racing across the desert. She was left to herself, to her thoughts, and the memories of her mother.

***

The house is silent. Night has fallen. She only returns because she is hungry. She worries about her father's reaction to her being gone so long. She hopes he is drunk enough to be asleep now. Aida only hopes her mother is in a forgiving mood since she hadn't returned from playing. She knew it was her mother who would be punished for her running away to hide in the tree line until the screaming stopped, until the giant was deep in slumber. She glances down at her dirty, torn dress. She runs her hands through her knotted hair and walks as softly as she can across the sitting room. The wooden floor threatens to give her away with its creaking but there is a voice upstairs, her mother is speaking. Her heart pounds and her hope of going unnoticed dies. Her father had to be awake if mother was speaking. Her mother learned not to talk too loudly or make very much noise once he had gone to bed, the consequences weren't worth it. Aida comes to the bottom stair and peers up at the silhouette of her mother.

"Never again, you bastard."

Aida holds her breath and considers retreating but when there isn't an explosive response to her mother's cursing, she knows something has happened to her father and somehow she's aware her life will never be the same.

"Don't be afraid, child."

Aida hesitates. Her mother is at the top of the steps, standing still but breathing heavily. She can only see her mother's figure outlined against the glow of a kerosene lamp on a small table behind her, there's something heavy and dripping in her right hand, and something long and pointed in her left.

"Never again, my little sparrow. He'll never hurt you or me again, remember this." Her mother's ragged voice breaks.

Her mother tosses the heavy, dripping object. It rolls down the stairs, thumping on every step, spattering Aida's little cheeks with warm liquid. It smells of copper, like wet rust. Even as a child, it didn't take much guessing as to what her mother threw down to her, not in a house where violence was an everyday occurrence. Her father's bloody head tumbled past her injured legs, staining her dress with droplets of his blood. His eyes stare wide, his mouth hangs open, and she can still smell the liquor on his dead tongue.

"Don't let any man break you, as he did me."

Her mother stumbles back, knocking the lamp over. She staggers down the stairwell, her breathing labored. A knife falls from her hand and lands on the steps. Aida recognizes it from the big wooden block in the kitchen where her mother would cut meat. Giant flesh cut as easily as a sow's. Aida holds her little hands out to brace her mother as she nearly falls at her feet. She clings desperately to the banister, each breath sounds like she's breathing through a wet cloth. Aida can see her now, her face as white as a sheet, but she's grinning. There is a bleeding hole in her chest, it runs red, a river of life flowing away. She is dying.

"I'm so sorry, Mama. I shouldn't have run away. I should've come inside, then everything would be normal like it was before." Aida weeps as her mother slumps down to sit on the stairs. Her head lulls over to rest against the splintered handrail.

"That's the problem, this was never normal, child."

A crackling sound drifts down the stairwell on a cloud of smoke. She looks up beyond the pitiful sight of her mother and sees a soft glow growing into a wild inferno.

"Go!" Her mother chokes, her lungs filling with blood and smoke.

Aida can hardly remember her feet carrying her outside, but she does recall her mother crying after her, "Fly away!"

***

All was still, quiet, and cold. Her eyes open, tears flooding them until she is blind. She feels a prickling running up the back of her neck. She can't stifle her cries. She pushes herself up and beats at the source of the sensation which to her felt like a spider or a scorpion crawling across her skin. Her commotion startles him awake. He sits upright, his silhouette is large and rigid, and he is cursing under his breath. Her stomach feels like a pit is opening up in it.

"Somethin' was on my neck."

He stands up and stomps over to her. Yanking her closer to him, she feels him breathe deeply. He used to pull her into him roughly but kiss her with a passion she'd never known. He pushes her back a bit and roughly begins inspecting her. She knows he felt the temptation too.

"Kiss me." She whispers and even in the near-perfect darkness she can see the anger building in him. Her reverie was the span of a heartbeat and yet felt eternal, the way they once were, it hurt to recall. To her they never sinned, only loved.

His hands turn violent as he brushes the sand from her dress and hair, ignoring her plea. "There's nothin' there!"

The prickling feeling traces its way down her body. She realizes it's the same static she felt when she heard her mother in the darkness.

"I swear, I felt it!"

"You're always so dramatic, why can't you just be normal?" he shoves her away.

"Normal?"

"Yes, like any other wife, normal." He raises his voice and his hand in the dark.

"None of this is normal."

"What'd you say?"

"None of this is normal!" she raises her voice, and she knows the outcome.

"Ungrateful bitch." his fist is a flash of sudden pain in the dark, rocking her head backwards. The world spins away from her.

She is a bride falling again, her veil drifting on the breeze. She is a bird caught in a deadly nosedive.

"This is over!" his voice is a growl, a giant's thunderous screaming.

She tastes blood and dirt in her mouth as she awakens face down in the sand. Her hearing is muffled by her heartbeat, but she can still hear him. He is bustling around in their gear, but her attention is drawn beyond their camp. The shadows are looming amidst the leaf bare trees, the vultures are watching, she is watching. Only the faintest outline, but it is her.

"Only one of us is leavin' this desert. I'll make a new life away from you, from what I used to be. I tried savin' you too, but you just wouldn't listen."

A shovel being driven into the earth beside her head punctuates his meaning.

Aida attempts to crawl away through the dust but the shovel sings through the air and connects with the back of her head. She falls forward and rolls onto her back. She holds her arms up, weakly attempting to stop his next assault.

"The wages of sin is death."

His silhouette, a beast ready to kill, is struck by a blur of black. John curses and steps back, a second, a third, a fourth blur of darkness swoops in. A cloud of black descends, screeching, it swarms over him. He falls, screaming but his voice is drowned in high pitched shrieking. A feather falls gently on Aida's cheek. Soft and black, smelling of decay.

"Get on your feet." Her mother's voice speaks.

Aida struggles to stand, at her feet lies the shovel he intended to bury her with. She stares down at John, a man who she knew was haunted by the ghost of who raised him, but he never knew she would be visited by a ghost of her own, one who intended to protect her at all costs.

"End your nightmare."

Aida lifts the shovel as the vultures flutter away. John is blind, his eyes taken in the frenzy. He reaches out to her, but she knows better, he is still a snake, a scorpion, a beast even when injured. She has dealt with his abuse too long to feel any forgiveness.

"Till death do you part." Her mother says.

Aida jabs the tip of the shovel downward with all her strength, it cuts into his throat and his blood sprays up onto her dress. He smells of wet rust and lies, of unforgiving brutality. She yanks the shovel free and immediately rams it back down into the gaping wound it already created until she feels it hit his spinal cord. She puts her foot on the back of the shovel and forces it downward until she feels it sever through to the blood-soaked sand on the other side.

***

The bride is adorned in a gown of dust. A veil of dried blood traces down her face and back in a train of crimson. She is following a procession of vultures gliding toward the outline of a distant city.

She has buried her past and her pain along with him. She is ready to fly.

WELCOME HOME

Jessica Guess

When Mom and me lived in Miami, the news was like a 24 hour Romero movie. Bath salted, zombie-like dudes eating human faces. Gator versus python deathmatches. Kilos of cocaine stuffed in pineapples. Florida Man. Man, oh man, Florida Man. I swear, Florida has a 'Welcome Home' beacon for all things morbid and monstrous this side of the world. Even in this stupid town, there was still chaos.

"Tonight, on Mount Dora evening news, a second girl has been kidnapped in as many weeks." The news anchor, Belkys Nerey, stared at me straight-faced from the TV screen in my living room. Her voice was low and serious, a stark change from her upbeat attitude during the 'Fun in the Sun' segment. "Authorities are still looking for information on a perpetrator."

My stomach growled loudly. There was nothing in the fridge. Nothing in the cupboards. My mom was working another late shift at the hospital, but if I was lucky, she'd get me something on her way back. Maybe I should have gotten something to eat after school. Taken the ten-minute walk across the bridge into town instead of the five-minute walk from the bus stop to our house on the other side of the river. But I didn't want to do that. I didn't want to get my own food. I wanted my mom to do it. I wanted to be a daughter again and not worry about what I was going to eat and when. Instead, all I got was hours and hours of pacing the small, tiled living room to the kitchen to look at a fridge filled with water and Sunny Delight and nothing else.

My stomach growled again. This time louder, locking my gut in a vice-like grip.

"Ugh." I held my belly with one hand and turned the volume up with the other.

"There is still no new information about the body found along the Dora shoreline earlier this month, but it has been established that it was *not* one of the missing girls," Belkys continued. Her jet-black hair was cut short with a swooped bang in the front. She had been an anchor down in Miami when we lived there. She'd left a year before we did. "If you remember, the body was found with its neck ripped out, eviscerated, and missing vital organs."

I shifted in my chair at the mention of evisceration. My parents were much better about that sort of thing. They could watch the goriest horror movie and eat the bloodiest cut of meat without flinching, but not me.

They showed the pictures of the missing girls again. One of them had creamy white skin, with strawberry blonde hair, and freckles on her fleshy cheeks. She looked close to my age, which meant she was also navigating the new terrain of high school freshman when she was abducted. The other girl was black, like me, but not as doughy around the middle. In her picture she was wearing a cheerleader's uniform. She was tall and lean and had skin a little darker than mine, but not by much, and her dark cotton candy hair was pulled back in two neat afro puffs.

A weird feeling made my stomach churn in a way that

had nothing to do with hunger. They were pretty, and it probably got them kidnapped and worse. Some psycho saw them, saw their faces, saw their bodies, and decided to…to what? Sometimes I just don't understand people.

I shifted on my couch again. It squeaked in a way that threatened to reveal the age of the old terry cloth and wood. My mom picked it up at the thrift store a week after we moved to town. We always moved around a lot but usually, we kept the same furniture. This time though, we left everything and bought "new" used stuff at garage sales and secondhand shops.

Mom wanted a change of pace. A fresh start. She had been wanting that more and more since Dad died. I kind of understood. Everything had been different since we lost him. Quieter. Lonelier. It really felt like it was just me and mom now. Us against the world.

That's why it sucked that she was so distant lately. She barely talked to me. She was always tired. We don't even eat together anymore. That used to be such a big thing for us. *All* of us.

Back then, when it was the three of us, mom and dad would either bring something home, or we'd go out to eat as a family. Dad would get the food and cut up my share for me while mom frowned at him.

"Vani needs to do it herself," she'd say.

"She's still a growing girl. Me helping her doesn't hurt," Dad would say, then wink at me and muss my hair.

I looked at the clock to see how late she was. *9:43.* She got off at 9. Maybe she really had gotten me some food on the way home. Maybe we'd eat together again like when Dad was here. Maybe I'd say something funny and she'd throw her head back in laughter, her thick kinky curls bouncing, a sliver of meat caught in her sharp teeth. My stomach growled again just as the front door slammed.

I jumped up from the sofa. "Mom?"

She didn't answer. Instead, she took off her shoes at the doorway and rubbed her feet. My mom has always been super pretty and strong. Her skin was deep brown, and she had muscular arms, dark striking eyes, high cheekbones, and full lips. She didn't look of this time. I did. I got her skin tone and her eyes, but that's about it. I've always been frumpy but not enough to be considered fat, and I'm half a foot shorter than my mom was at my age.

All the hormones in our food, Dad used to assure me when I'd complain. *Don't worry, baby. You'll grow soon enough.*

"You bring anything to eat?" I asked.

She looked at me, confused. "What? You haven't eaten yet?"

"No," I said. "I was waiting on you. I thought we'd—"

"Vanessa." She sighed my name like the burden I was. "I need you to be more considerate, okay? I can't do everything by myself. It's hard enough now that we're all alone."

"We're not alone."

She blinked at me. "What?"

"We're not alone. You shouldn't say things like that."

She inhaled deeply and made her way to the sofa. She sat down and crossed her legs like one of those actresses in a black and white movie.

"Lena Horne," an old landlord had said to us when my

dad was still around. "You look like Lena Horne. Taller and broader shoulders, but pretty just the same. Especially the teeth."

My mom and dad smiled at each other then at the old man's compliment. She smiled a lot more back then. When Dad was still here. When we were still looking for others.

"If you want to get you hopes up, Vani, go right ahead. Don't expect me to."

It was the first time she said it so concretely. The first time she really sounded like she had given up.

"If Dad was here—"

"He's not." Her eyes flashed, for a second showing their true color before returning to deep brown. "It's hard enough without you reminding me what he'd say every other second. I *know* what he'd say. But he's not here. Like it or not it's just you and me and we *are* all alone. I need you to grow up."

Her words hit me right in my chest. Red hot anger swelled in my stomach and churned along with the hunger. "Fine," I said and grabbed my jacket and keys.

She turned from the couch to watch me "Where are you going?"

"To get something to eat. Some of the stores in town are open til 10:30."

"It's too late."

I turned to her. "I'm a grown-up, right?"

She glared at me but didn't say anything. She turned away and I did the same.

***

Most people who aren't from Florida wouldn't believe that it gets chilly here. It does. Especially in February when the temperature can drop below 60 or even 50. I wouldn't go as far as to call that cold. That would be an insult. Especially after that time we lived in Minnesota. I wrapped my arms around myself at the memory of it. I still don't know what my parents were thinking. We hate the cold. We were supposedly looking for family, but we didn't end up finding anyone and moved back to the south after only three months. Three snowy, ice-cold months.

I zipped my jacket up to my neck and quickened my pace. If I was fast enough, maybe I could make it to my favorite place.

Like it or not it's just you and me and we are all alone. I need you to grow up.

How could she say that? How could she believe it? For one, we *weren't* alone. We had each other. It kind of hurt that I wasn't enough for her. For two, I knew that there were others like us out there. Others who had lost loved ones the way we lost Dad. Others who hunted like us. Others who ate like us.

I was so engrossed in my thoughts that I wasn't paying attention to my surroundings. I was thinking about Dad and what happened that night we were caught eating. How those people from that stupid farmer town surrounded us, blood still on our faces, Mom still picking that girl out of her second row of teeth. How I slowed my parents down. How I couldn't fight off that man with the axe. How Dad bit into the man's arm and told me to run. How my father screamed as the axe's blade found his skull.

My ears were filled with my father's last yell, so I

didn't hear the vehicle's engine. I didn't hear the wheels slowing down as it got closer, but I did see the headlights illuminating the black pavement in front of me. I turned my head just enough to make out the pale blue van, then a pair of hands were on me, grabbing me around my waist and pulling me into a doorway to darkness.

My jaw slammed against the floor, smashing my mouth shut. Blood flooded my mouth, the coppery sweetness welcomed on my hungry tongue.

"Go, go, go!" A male voice belonging to the hands shouted and I felt the van accelerate.

"She pretty?" another male voice called from the driver's seat.

"Pretty enough," the first man said.

I screamed and punched wildly. I kicked and tried to edge away but the man's huge fist met my stomach, knocking the wind out of me. I coughed twice and spat blood

Those two missing girls from the news flashed in my mind. I was like them. I would be a picture on the news tomorrow. But then, there was another story.

The body. Eviscerated. Vital organs missing. Another face flashed in my head. It was the man with the axe who I still saw in my nightmares. My dad's scream. My mother's horror. My mother's disgust.

I need you to grow up.

She was right. I was weak, and it cost us Dad. I couldn't be weak anymore. I couldn't leave my mom all alone.

With barely a thought, my second row of teeth descended. I bit the man's neck taking a chunk of flesh out, chewed twice, and swallowed. Blood spurted onto my face, onto the van's walls, onto the floor, and the man jumped back and held his neck. He sputtered and tried to scream but half his throat was torn away.

"Oh, no," I said, eyeing the wound.

I'd severed his jugular. A stupid mistake. A *child's* mistake. One my mother would never make. It's why I liked when she and Dad did the hunting. They knew just how to bite into the prey's neck so that they couldn't scream but were still alive long enough for us to enjoy our meal. Dad always loved the liver. I'd get one of the lungs. Mom always ate last because she liked to eat the heart up until its last beat.

My claws descended when my teeth did, and I used them to rip into the right side of the man's chest.

"Avoid the heart. That has to be last," my Dad told me the one time I took lead on a hunt.

I tore past flesh and muscle while the man gurgled and flailed weakly beneath me. His insides felt warm and tender. My mouth watering, I pulled out a lung and bit into it, but what was supposed to be raw and succulent was burned and tasted of chemicals.

A smoker.

I gagged and spat out the disgusting meat. That's why I prefer children. Sure, their organs are smaller, but for the most part, they're untainted by hormones, medications, and unnatural chemicals. If it weren't for this man, I'd be at Toys R Us now, luring a child away. Promising a toy or candy.

My would-be rapist was twitching in his last moments of life, now useless to me, but I had another chance. I got down on all fours and made my way to the black curtain that blocked the front of the van from view. I focused my ears and heard his fast, erratic heartbeat. His breathing had a slight wheeze to it.

Ugh, another smoker.

But this one wasn't as bad as the first. His lungs sounded only slightly tainted. Not ideal, but it would do for now. My stomach growled again, teased by the promise of food. I ripped the curtain away.

"Hey, how was—" He stopped mid-sentence after seeing my now yellow eyes in the rearview mirror. He screamed, and that's when I saw it. The look that they all get when they see us. Eyes wide, mouth slackened, unable to conjure the slightest of sounds. They can't comprehend beings as ancient as us. My mother's mother lived for three-hundred years. Her mother before her for seven-hundred. It's how we're built. Human to the naked eye until we feed and then our real sets of teeth descend from behind our disguise ones. Our skin thickens until its near-impenetrable all over except for our skulls. Our talons grow from our fingertips, sharp enough to claw through steel. Our yellow eyes glow, cat-like with vertical slits for pupils. We must be hideous to them, but not as much as they are to me.

I clawed into his shoulders. He reached back and grabbed a fist full of my hair, ripping some of it out. I screamed but bit down into the side of his neck, making sure to miss the jugular like my father told me. The man yelled again and swerved the van wildly as I ripped out his flesh. He reached back again, trying to push my face away, but his hand landed near my mouth. I chomped down on his thumb, biting it off and swallowing it whole.

I didn't notice we were veering off the road until it was too late. The van crashed into a ditch on the side of the road, throwing me and the man through the windshield of the car.

I covered my face right before I went through the glass and thankfully a pile of mud softened my landing. Glass and dirt covered my hair and arms, but I was okay. No real damage to my skull.

I rolled over and looked up at the night sky, breathing hard and in a slight daze. I laid there for a minute, the wet mud making my clothes stick to my hardened skin. A few feet away, the man whimpered and brought me back to my senses. I got up and made my way to him. He was trying his best to crawl away, crying now, holding his neck with his thumb-less hand and sputtering. When we'd crashed, I'd heard something in his spine sever. His legs were useless. I made to pin him down on his stomach so I could better reach the lung but stopped short.

Maybe I'll try the heart this time.

You have to be really good to eat it the way my mother does, so that it is still beating as you're eating. Only the best of our kind can do it. I'd never done it before. A wave of nervousness coursed through me.

This is good practice.

I rolled the man over. He covered his face with his bloody hand and tried to scream but only blood spurted from the wound.

"Shut up," I said as I bent over him.

I tore into the man's chest and broke open his rib cage. He made more gurgling noises as I worked, carefully using my index claw to snip away muscle and sinew. I peeled open the tiny membrane surrounding the beating organ and touched it. Lungs usually felt firm and beefy and took long to chew, this felt softer. His heart felt as if it could melt apart in my fingers if I held it too long and when I bit into it, the last few beats thumping against my lips, the meat was so tender it nearly melted in my mouth.

Blood dripped from my mouth and onto the man's already reddened shirt. On it was a huge golden sun, now ripped in half with the words, "Welcome to Florida" written across it.

I laughed. You should see me now, Mom. I'm learning. And when we find more of our kind, I'll show them how grown up I am. How I can eat like you do.

THE BODY YOU LOVED

Gemma Amor

Here is the body you loved, lying still upon the bed
Sleeping? No, not in the truest sense, but dead
My eyes sealed to your pain (thank god)
Mouth closed, no kisses, not now
Beautiful, nonetheless, reposed
Clear features, no troubled frown

Here is the body you loved, growing cool, a fire died
down
The heart that beat within, no further future to be found
This is the hair you stroked (my hair)
Cool as nature's reproach
Remember the times you wound it around my throat?
Careful, of decay's approach

Here is the body *I* loved, I left it as you dreamed
You woke to find me gone, rolled into me and screamed
This is the skin you bit (my skin)
Hard now as crackled glaze
A spasm, life left without fanfare
But it's only been three days

Stop holding the body you loved, my love
Stop rocking me that way
I am gone, sweetheart, and I can't come back
I am gone to a different place

But the way you loved, and the way you mourn
Are the things that keep me whole
As I drift above and watch you cry
A watchful, anchored soul

And the body you loved will lie in the soil
And the body you fucked will corrode
And the body you shared will make food for the worms
And for you, the stars will implode
But the things we love and the time we had
Are never really ours to own
You must remember this my love
That my body was my home
And you filled it with good, warm, living things
And you wrapped it tight with care
And you made my body a thing of joy
And the stars, in time,
Will repair.

AUTHOR BIOS

Cynthia "Cina" Pelayo is the author of LOTERIA, SANTA MUERTE, THE MISSING, and POEMS OF MY NIGHT, all of which have been nominated for International Latino Book Awards. POEMS OF MY NIGHT was also nominated for an Elgin Award. CHILDREN OF CHICAGO will be released by Agora Books on 2/9/21. Cina was raised in inner city Chicago, where she lives with her husband and children. Find her online at http://cinapelayo.com and on Twitter as @cinapelayo.

Gemma Amor is the Bram Stoker Award nominated author of Dear Laura, White Pines, Girl on Fire and Cruel Works of Nature, amongst other works. She is also a podcaster, illustrator and voice actor, and is based in Bristol in the U.K. Many of her stories have been adapted into audio dramas by the wildly popular NoSleep Podcast, and her work also features on shows like Shadows at the Door, Creepy, and The Grey Rooms. She is the co-creator, writer and voice actor for horror-comedy podcast Calling Darkness, which stars Kate Siegel, and was also nominated for a This is Horror and Ladies of Horror Fiction award in 2019. Heavily influenced by classical literature, gothic romance, tragedy and heroism, she is most at home in front of a fire with a single malt and a dog-eared copy of anything by Angela Carter. Find her at gemmaamorauthor.com or @manylittlewords on Twitter.

Laurel Hightower grew up in Kentucky, attending college in California and Tennessee before returning home to horse country, where she lives with her husband, son and two rescue animals. She works as a paralegal in a mid-size firm, wrangling litigators by day and writing at night. A bourbon and beer girl, she's a fan of horror movies and true life ghost stories, and is one third of the Ink Heist podcast team. She is the author of Whispers in the Dark and Crossroads, and has several pieces of short fiction slated for publication in various upcoming anthologies.

Sarah Read is a dark fiction writer. Her short stories can be found in various places, including Ellen Datlow's Best Horror of the Year volumes 10 and 12. A collection of her short fiction called OUT OF WATER is available from Trepidatio Publishing, as is her debut novel THE BONE WEAVER'S ORCHARD, both nominated for the Bram Stoker, This is Horror, and Ladies of Horror Fiction Awards. THE BONE WEAVER'S ORCHARD won the Stoker for Superior Achievement in a First Novel and the This Is Horror Award for Novel of the Year. You can find her online on Instagram or Twitter @inkwellmonster or on her site at www.inkwellmonster.wordpress.com.

S.H. Cooper is a Florida based author who has penned short stories, novellas and novels, co-wrote the podcast Calling Darkness, and is a regular contributor to award-winning anthology series the NoSleep Podcast. When not writing, she enjoys spending time with her husband, pets, and a cup of Earl Grey.

Hailey Piper is the author of horror novellas Benny Rose, the Cannibal King, The Possession of Natalie Glasgow, and The Worm and His Kings. She is a member of the HWA and her short fiction appears in Daily Science Fiction, The Arcanist, Year's Best Hardcore Horror, Volume 5, and elsewhere. She lives with her wife in Maryland, where they eat Old Bay by day and bay at the moon by night. Find her on Twitter via @HaileyPiperSays or at www.haileypiper.com.

Sara Tantlinger is the author of the Bram Stoker Award-winning The Devil's Dreamland: Poetry Inspired by H.H. Holmes, and the Stoker-nominated novella To Be Devoured. Her other works include Love For Slaughter, The Devil's City written with Matt Corley, Cradleland of Parasites, and she edited the anthology Not All Monsters. Along with being a mentor for the HWA Mentorship Program, she is also a co-organizer for the HWA Pittsburgh Chapter. She embraces all things macabre and can be found lurking in graveyards or on Twitter @SaraTantlinger and at saratantlinger.com

J. Danielle Dorn is the author of Devil's Call, a Kirkus 'Must-Read Science Fiction, Fantasy & Horror Book' from Inkshares. Their short fiction has appeared in or on Ink Heist, Tough Crime, Witch Craft Magazine, and

Monsters Out of the Closet, as well as Madness Heart Press's Trigger Warning series. A military brat and former mental health paraprofessional, they currently live in Rochester, NY with their cat and not enough bookshelves.

Eve Harms is a writer of freaky, fun dark fiction. Her work has appeared in the Vastarien Literary Journal (under Rayna Waxhead), Creepy Catalog (under Kendra Temples), and her story 'The Glow at Home' was featured on Ellen Datlow's recommended list in the anthology Best Horror of the Year Vol. 11. She currently resides in Los Angeles with her children's book illustrator spouse and two cats. You can find her at eveharms.com or on Twitter and Instagram under @eveharmswrites.

Sonora Taylor is the award-winning author of Little Paranoias: Stories, Without   Condition, Seeing Things, The Crow's Gift and Other Tales, and Wither and Other Stories. Her short stories frequently appear in The Siren's Call. Her work has been published by Camden Park Press, Cemetery Gates Media, Kandisha Press, Tales to Terrify, and others. She lives in Arlington, Virginia, with her husband and a rescue dog.

Beverley Lee is the bestselling author of the Gabriel Davenport vampire suspense series (The Making of Gabriel Davenport, A Shining in the Shadows and The Purity of Crimson) and the gothic horror, The Ruin of

Delicate Things. In thrall to the written word from an early age, especially the darker side of fiction, she believes that the very best story is the one you have to tell. You can visit her at www.beverleylee.com) or on Instagram (@theconstantvoice) and Twitter (@constantvoice).

Violet Castro is a Mexican American writer originally from Texas now residing in the UK with her family. She writes horror, science fiction, erotica, and erotic horror. Violet is also the co-founder of www.frightgirlsummer.com , a website dedicated to women in dark fiction with an emphasis on women from marginalized communities. For More information about her books and other publications, please visit www.vvcastro.com. You can also follow her on Twitter and Instagram @vlatinalondon.

Red Lagoe grew up on eighties horror and carried her paranoia for slashers and sewer creatures into adulthood. She is a staff writer for the shared-world short fiction series, Still Water Bay. Her stories have been published by Crystal Lake Publishing, Perpetual Motion Machine Publishing, Sinister Smile Press, and more. Red's collection Lucid Screams released in February 2020. When she's not spewing her horror-ridden mind onto the page, she can be found substituting at an elementary school or dabbling in amateur astronomy. Find more by Red at www.redlagoe.com.

Cassie Daley is a blogger, artist, and writer living in Northern California with her boyfriend and three dogs. Her first published short story, 'Ready or Not', debuted on Fright Girl Summer. Aside from writing, she runs an online art shop and contributes to the Ladies of Horror Fiction website. She is the creator of THE BIG BOOK OF HORROR AUTHORS: A Coloring & Activity Book, and is also a host on The PikeCast, a book podcast dedicated to reading and discussing the works of Christopher Pike. You can find Cassie on Twitter as @ctrlaltcassie, or letsgetgalactic.com.

Erin Sweet Al-Mehairi is an author, editor, journalist, advocate, and publicist with twenty-five years' experience in communication fields. She's been putting pen to paper for over thirty years. Breathe. Breathe was her debut collection of dark poetry and short stories. She is featured in several anthologies, online magazines, and was co-editor of a Gothic anthology. Born in England, she now mothers three busy teens and a spoiled cat in a forest in Ohio while running her Hook of a Book business. Find Erin at www.hookofabook.wordpress.com/, Amazon, and GoodReads.

Sadie Hartmann aka 'Mother Horror' reviews horror fiction for several platforms and publications including Cemetery Dance and SCREAM Magazine. You can find her columns and articles at Tor Nightfire and LitReactor.

She is the co-owner of the horror fiction subscription company, Night Worms. Sadie lives in the beautiful PNW with her husband of 20+ years where they enjoy perfect weather, street tacos, and hanging out with their three kids. They have a Frenchie named Owen.

Lilyn George is the owner of Sci-Fi & Scary (https://www.scifiandscary.com/), a genre-focused reviews and entertainment site that hosts a multinational team of writers. They identify as nonbinary, bisexual, and atheist.

Amanda McHugh is a writer from upstate NY. Her works have appeared in various literary magazines and podcasts, most notably the award-winning NoSleep Podcast. When she's not writing, Mandy enjoys baking too many cookies and planning adventures for her family. She lives in Upstate NY with her husband, two kids, and goofy dog.

Michelle Garza and Melissa Lason have been dubbed the 'Sisters of Slaughter' for their work in the horror and dark fantasy genres. Their work has been published by Thunderstorm Books, Sinister Grin Press, Bloodshot Books, and Death's Head Press. Their debut novel, Mayan Blue, was nominated for a Bram Stoker award.

Jessica Guess is a writer and English teacher who hails

from Fort Lauderdale, Florida. She earned her Creative Writing MFA from Minnesota State University, Mankato in 2018 and is the founder of the website Black Girl's Guide to Horror where she examines horror movies in terms of quality and intersectionality. Her creative work has been featured in Luna Station Quarterly and Tor Nightfire. Her debut novella, Cirque Berserk, is available for purchase on Amazon. Her short story, "The Nightmare Man," will be released in Shiver: A Cold Weather Horror Anthology in January.

ACKNOWLEDGEMENTS

An endeavor such as this cannot be brought into being without the help of many, and as such, we, Laurel, Gemma and Cina, would like to offer our heartfelt thanks to the following people:

To Burial Day Books and Gerardo Pelayo for the wisdom, expertise, hard work and a home for this book to spring from, as well as providing the paperback contributor copies.

To Kealan Patrick Burke for contributing his considerable skill in the lettering and wraparound for the cover.

To Karmen Wells for her generosity and brilliant line editing - we all learned so much from you.

To each of the authors in this volume – as a charity anthology, every story and poem was donated without pay, and given the skill and subject matter that bleeds onto these pages, that's no small ask. We thank you for giving so freely of your time and yourselves. You are here in this book and we are so very proud of what you have helped us to accomplish.

Thank you to those authors who read advanced copies and provided blurbs that both increased the visibility of this book and lifted our hearts. Brian Keene, Kathe Koja, Gabino Iglesias, Josh Malerman and everyone else who accepted advance copies and helped us spread the word:

thank you for your support.

To our wonderful horror community – the whirlwind of immediate excitement and kindness that began from our first announcement of this anthology has been both humbling and exhilarating. When our energy has flagged, you've given us renewed life.

And to the women. All women. We see you, we honor you, we are you. Tell your stories, refuse to be silenced, and run with the pack.

Printed in Great Britain
by Amazon